PUFFIN BOOKS

GAFFER SAMSON'S LUCK

James can't believe his parents have chosen such a flat and boring piece of the countryside for their new home. The fen country feels like 'nowhere' after the 'somewhere' of Yorkshire and when James goes to the local school it seems that the inhabitants are as hostile as the land itself. Excluded by the village children because he is new and too clever, his only friend is Angey, the cheeky but likeable little tinker. And then there's old Gaffer Samson, ill in bed in the next-door cottage who befriends James and asks him to try and find his 'luck' – an old gypsy charm he was given years before.

The search for the luck leads James into confrontation with 'the village', the local school gang he can never be part of. A way out of the isolation presents itself in the form of a dangerous dare. What began as a simple task to help the Gaffer, turns into a life and death drama in which James must prove himself in order to survive . . .

Jill Paton Walsh has written many highly acclaimed books for children. She has previously won the Whitbread Award and the Universe Literary Prize for *A Parcel of Patterns*, and *Gaffer Samson's Luck* was the Grand Prix winner of the Smarties Prize in 1985.

Gaffer Samson's Luck

Jill Paton Walsh

Illustrated by Brock Cole

PUFFIN BOOKS

PUFFIN BOOKS

Published by the Penguin Group
Penguin Books Ltd, 27 Wrights Lane, London W8 5TZ, England
Penguin Books USA Inc., 375 Hudson Street, New York, New York 10014, USA
Penguin Books Australia Ltd, Ringwood, Victoria, Australia
Penguin Books Canada Ltd, 2801 John Street, Markham, Ontario, Canada L3R 1B4
Penguin Books (NZ) Ltd, 182–190 Wairau Road, Auckland 10, New Zealand

Penguin Books Ltd, Registered Offices: Harmondsworth, Middlesex, England

First published in the U.S.A. by Farrar, Straus & Giroux 1984
First published in Great Britain by Viking Kestrel 1985
Published in Puffin Books 1987
3 5 7 9 10 8 6 4

Text copyright © Jill Paton Walsh, 1984
Illustrations copyright © Brock Cole
All rights reserved

Printed in England by Clays Ltd, St Ives plc
Typeset in Bembo

For Jessica, very early;
and Clare, very late

'We can't be nearly there,' said James, from the back seat of the car. 'Here isn't anywhere. It's been nowhere for miles!'

'What do you mean, James?' asked his father, driving, with an edge to his voice.

'No up and no down,' said James, 'and no trees. Nothing.'

'It's the Fens,' his father said.

'But when we get there, Dad, please, Dad, there will be something, won't there? We're not going to live on this? Dad?'

'We're going to live where we can, James,' his father said. 'Belt up.'

James looked out of the side window of the car. He saw ten level miles or more; no slopes, no trees, a green ditch on a black field, glinting red, as though ruled on the land with a Dayglo pencil, pointing straight at the setting sun, which glowered at him naked, just above the rim of the land.

His mother spoke to them both. To James she said, 'There was no work for your father in the Dales, James. There's a good job in Peterborough.'

'We could move to Peterborough. That's a place. There would be houses in the way of seeing this.'

'We shall be near enough to Cambridge, too. There will be other jobs if this one folds.'

To James's father she said, 'It's all right. He's only a

little boy, and it's the first time he's had to move. He'll settle.'

'He must, we must,' James's father said. 'I don't like it either.'

'We all will in time,' his mother said. 'Let's just get there.'

But long before they got there, James was fast asleep.

He woke in a room full of light. He was lying under a white painted slope, which at first he thought was pink and gold; then he realized it was reflecting very early light which shone softly on it through uncurtained windows. He was sleeping on a mattress on the floor, in his pyjamas, though he could not remember getting into them. His clothes lay tossed on one of three packing-cases standing at the other end of the room. It was a long low attic with a dormer on one side and two skylights on the other. The stairs came up in the middle of the room with a banister rail round them. James got up at once and looked out of a skylight. He could see a line of rooftops and a lot of trees. Somehow the attic skylight was looking out behind a row of houses, as though it was not part of the street, but tucked away at an angle. The trees were in people's gardens. Tile and thatch and chimney-pots; a cedar of Lebanon, and vast towering spreading beech tree; three poplars and the top of a weeping willow ... James was pleased. This looked like somewhere. He could see between one tall tree and another a slender church spire a little distance off. Then he looked the other way, through the dormer window. A few new houses. A stump of brick – a windmill with neither roof nor sails.

Just beyond it the plate-glass windows of what was obviously the school; and beyond that nowhere again.

Under a lemon gold sky the land was black; and nothing put a stop to it. Far away on his right he could just see a line of very slight upslope; he could not call it hill. In every other direction the land ran on and on until it melted, blurred away. Before his line of vision was blocked by anything his strength of sight ran out, leaving him squinting at the horizon. In the distance he saw four more church spires. But it would have taken hundreds to fill such a vast space to a pleasant degree. And it made James feel dizzy, and unprotected, as though he were standing all crumpled and sleepy in a public place.

He sat down and considered the attic. He liked it, in itself. All it wanted was to be in Yorkshire, and he would have liked it a lot. He could put his stereo the other side of the stairs from his bed, and hang his model aeroplane from the ceiling. And if he put the bed under the skylight he would be able to lie on his back at night and look straight up at the sky. He tried it, lying on the floor, beside a packing-case, and at once saw birds skimming the roof, brushing the glass; he even heard the light dry scuffle of a wing feather. A considerable racket of birds was going on outside, he realized; perhaps that was what had woken him, rather than the light.

Then it occurred to him that nobody had promised him the attic. Perhaps it wouldn't be his; perhaps there was an ordinary room for him somewhere else. He had been too cross at moving to ask anything, or listen to anything about it. He picked up his shoes, and went down the stairs to explore.

Down the attic stair he found first a narrow landing, with three doors. One door was shut – doubtless James's parents were asleep behind that – and one was the bathroom. James glanced swiftly into the third bedroom, and hoped once more for the attic. Downstairs there wasn't much to find. A long narrow sitting-room, and a long narrow kitchen, sink at one end, table and dresser at the other. Sunshine poured in and diamonded the chrome taps. There was hardly space to turn round in either room. James sighed. How could his parents possibly have chosen this rabbit hutch? He went to get himself a drink from the tap, picking up a mug full of sawdust from one of the packing-cases, and saw, as he did so, an intruder in the back garden.

An old man was standing outside the back window of the kitchen, his back turned to James, seemingly just standing there, staring. James unbolted the back door and shot out through it.

'What are you doing in our garden?' he demanded. But he found himself standing on a gravel path, that ran the length of the long row of cottages, between the back doors and little fenced-off patches of garden.

'Oi'm not in your garden, though, boy,' the man said. 'Oi'm on the righter way. Oi've the right, you've the right, all them what lives in the whole row got the right. On foot or with a barrer to come and go by.'

'Oh,' said James. 'Sorry. Isn't this bit ours?' He waved at the neatly planted little patch nearest to his back door.

'Thass mine, bor. Yew new in number two, are yew? Then thass your'n, over there.'

James looked at a tiny piece of grass, all overgrown,

and a thick tall row of leggy roses. At the back of the patch was a broken and sagging shed.

'It's small, isn't it?' said James, sorrowfully.

'Thass not very big,' the man said. 'There's a vegetable plot goes with yours, down the path to the end, along of mine.'

'Oh,' said James. He trotted down the path, to look. The path ran along the back of the row, past little sentry-box porches, painted black, to a set of allotments at the end. James supposed theirs must be the one with nothing on it except dead Brussels sprouts. He trotted back. The man was still outside, staggering under the weight of a coal scuttle.

'Can I carry that for you?' said James. He looked properly at the man. He had big, sagging features, and tousled grey hair. Little brushes of grey hair grew out of his ears. All his clothes seemed loose, and he stooped a little. He was wearing carpet slippers that bulged in shapes not much like feet.

'Oi dunno,' the man said. 'Can yew?'

James picked up the coal scuttle and carried it through the next-door back door. 'Dew you put it down on the hearth, bor,' the man said.

The room looked very old fashioned to James. It was all brown and cream and faded, and it had a bed in it, as well as downstairs things. He put the scuttle down on the hearth, beside the glowing fire.

'Thankee,' the man said. 'Now, wass your name, bor?'

'James. What's yours?'

'Mr Samson, I am. But everybody calls me Gaffer. Been called Gaffer for fifty year.'

'Are you too old to go upstairs to bed, Gaffer?' said James.

'Yuss. Yuss, I am,' the Gaffer said. 'But I got enough sense to put me clothes on afore I goo out in the morning!'

'Oh, heck!' said James, realizing he was still in his pyjamas, and fled.

'Crab sandwiches,' James's mother was saying. 'Oh, there you are, James. I can manage crab sandwiches, but there doesn't seem to be anything else for breakfast.'

'With coffee?' said James's father.

'Coffee, yes. Morning papers, no.'

'BBC News?'

'If you feel like unpacking the tea-chest in the bedroom for the radio. You could always talk to your wife and son over breakfast.'

'So I could. Well, son, how do you like the new place?'

'It's very small,' said James, cautiously.

'Cosy. Your mother prefers cosy to small. Anything else?'

'It doesn't seem to have a proper garden. There was an old man getting coal where our garden ought to be.'

'You're getting a bit old to kick footballs in gardens. Anything else?'

'I like the attic,' said James.

'We thought you would. It's yours. O.K.?'

'Triffic!' said James. 'Can I put things just where I want?'

'Just where you want. Look, I think I'd better be off. I don't know how long it takes to get to Peterborough yet, and I mustn't be late while I'm still new. Be good, James. Bye, love.'

James's father put his coat on, and picked up his brief-case, and then came back to the table and swilled the rest of his coffee standing up, before disappearing through the back door.

'Can I have another funny sandwich, Mum?' said James. 'And, Mum? Have we gone poor?'

'Poor?' said James's mother. 'Gracious, no, James! We're rich! Poor doesn't mean living in a small place, it means not having a place at all. It means having to say no when your son wants a second sandwich. Not having enough clothes. Not knowing where to find the money to keep yourself warm. We're a million miles from poor, James.' She put a thick brown sandwich on his plate, and sat down opposite him at the table.

'James, I like this funny little place. When we have put a bit of paint on it, and unpacked all our pretty things, it will be charming. It used to be a malting: it wasn't built as houses, that's why our bit is so narrow and high. They used to sprout and roast barley here, for making beer, and it had three storeys, and lots of little windows. Then they divided it into cottages, and filled in the windows, and put new ones in different places; that's why the walls are all patterned and patched. Where the yard was once, where the wagons of barley drove in, the tenants in the cottages dug out little gardens, piecemeal, higgledy-piggledy. It's very different from a Yorkshire rectory, James, but in its different way it's very nice. Give it a chance, will you?'

James sat and glared at his sandwich. He didn't feel

like eating it any more, and he knew better than to say so.

His mother got up and began to wash up. 'I think there are some shops right here in the village, James. If I give you a list, will you find them and do some shopping for me? Then we'll unpack the tea-chests, and we'll start with your things if you like.'

James found a funny little thatched shop where he could buy shelf paper, and, he noticed, jigsaw puzzles, drawing books, crayons, rubbers and suchlike. He found the Post Office – very easy, that one, with a bright red pillar-box mounted on the wall – and bought stamps and envelopes. There was a sweet shop actually joined on to James's own house, the very end of the terrace, facing on to the street, and beyond it a butcher and greengrocer and grocer all in one, where most of the things on his mother's list would be.

Outside the big shop a small thin girl was standing. As James passed her she said, 'Buy us a Mars bar.'

James stared at her. 'Why should I?' he said. She was wearing a T-shirt and a thin cotton skirt, and she looked very goose-pimpled and bluish round the lips, as one would expect, considering how cold a day it was. She was also very dirty: James saw a grimy watermark on her neck.

'I got the money,' she said. 'I wasn't asking for money. Just, will yer get it for me?'

'If you've got the money,' said James, 'why not get it yourself?'

She pointed at a card, neatly lettered in block capitals,

stuck in the glass of the shop door. NO VAN DWELLERS,
it said.

'That's me,' she said. 'They won't serve me, see?'

'Well, that's not fair,' said James. The girl shrugged,
and held out her money in a grimy hand.

'All right,' said James, taking it. He worked his way
round the shelves in the shop, with his mother's list,
finding it all. Then he picked up a Mars bar, and queued
to pay. Two women ahead of him spent ages talking to
the girl at the till about the weather, so he took what

seemed like hours to get out of the shop, but the girl was still waiting for him outside.

'You shouldn't eat Mars bars,' he said, giving it to her. 'They're bad for your teeth.'

'Not if they're your dinner, they ain't,' she said. 'It's me dinner, this is. Can't be bad for me.'

'It just is bad for you,' said James. 'You should buy something sensible for dinner.'

'With 20p?' she said. 'Leave off!'

'Oh,' said James. 'What does it mean, "Van dwellers"? You can't live in a van.'

'Mobile home, down the trailer park,' she said. 'Caravans. That sorter van. Course I can.'

'Oh,' said James again.

'I'm Angey,' she said. 'Who're you?'

'James.'

'Visiting?'

'Come to live.'

'See yer, then.'

'I'll see you at school, I expect,' said James, realizing as he said it that Angey might not be the best choice of first friend in a new place.

'Not if I can help it!' she said, skipping away suddenly down a narrow little path between houses.

But when James, having sat politely through an interview with the Headmistress, was finally ushered into a classroom, Angey was there, right at the back. It was a very quiet classroom, with a grey-haired teacher in charge. All the children at all the tables stared at James. James pretended not to mind. Miss Dean found him a place at a table, well away from Angey. They were doing maths. James began to work his way down the page of sums. They weren't very hard. He did them all. When he had finished, James put up his hand.

'Yes, James?' said Miss Dean.

'What shall I do now?' said James.

'Keep doing the sums,' she said.

'I've finished them,' said James.

'Show me,' said Miss Dean. James trotted up to the front with his paper, and showed her.

'Well, you'll just have to sit and wait for the others to finish,' she said.

James was amazed. At his other school, if you finished early you were allowed to go and work in the nature corner, or do a drawing. He went back to his place and sat down. He could hear the scratching of pencils all around him, and someone whispering till Miss Dean looked that way. He looked at the classroom walls. There were some drawings pinned up, and a chart of the nine-times table. Through the huge windows of the classroom he could see a vast spread of land. It was entirely flat. Winter wheat made it blaze in unlikely green. A row of willow trees crossed the view a great way off. A shadow spire on a distant church rose above them. A man and a dog walked along the edge of a ditch. James thought at first they were moving unnaturally slowly; then he realized that it just seemed slowly, with nothing anywhere near them to mark how far they had travelled; they were just in the view, and if they kept walking along that field they would be in the view all morning.

James sighed. Then in desperation he opened the maths book again and began to work the sums from the next chapter along the margins of his paper. At once Miss Dean was standing behind his chair.

'What are you doing?' she said. 'If you do tomorrow's work now, what do you think you are going to do tomorrow, may I ask? I told you to wait for the others. Just wait.'

But at that moment the bell rescued James. It was morning break.

James stood a while near the fence in the playground. A game was being played on the tarmac between the school building and the road. It looked like catch and tag. James thought that was rather babyish, but everyone seemed to join in. He marched across to the crowd of children, and said, 'Can I play?'

A big girl with plaits seemed to be in charge. 'I don't know,' she said. 'Just moved here, have you?'

'Last week.'

'But you're village, aren't you? This game is all estate.'

'What's estate?' asked James.

'He can't be estate, Joanne,' another girl piped up. 'Nobody's moved out since last term. And nobody's moved in.'

'That's the estate,' the girl called Joanne told him. She waved her arm at the houses across the road. Row after row of neat modern houses stood there. A line of council semis along the road, and behind them glimpses of the white-boarded and plate-glass fronts of newer houses.

'He could be from near Mark's house,' a boy said.

'Are you?' demanded Joanne.

'I don't know where Mark's house *is*!' said James. 'I've only been here a few days.'

'There's a row of big new houses in the middle of the village, up Church Lane,' she said. 'Those count as estate.'

'I'm not in one of those,' said James. 'I'm in a malting that was, just off the High Street, by the sweet shop.'

'The Terrace,' she said. 'That's village.'

'O.K.,' said James. 'So it's village. Can I play?'

'Not if you're village,' said Joanne. 'We don't like them, and they don't like us.'

James shrugged, and plodded round the school building to the other side. There was another playground there, between the building and the open fields. There wasn't a game on this one; some little girls were chanting and skipping, and a little boy was bouncing a ball and counting his catches; the bigger children were all standing round in a huddle, talking.

James plodded up to them.

'No, you don't,' said a boy half his size. 'You lot play the other side.'

'I'm not estate,' said James. 'I've moved into the terrace by the sweet shop.'

The group parted, so that James could see a hefty big boy in the middle, smoking a cigarette. This boy stared at James from under a thatch of unkempt red hair. 'Please, Miss, can I have more sums!' he crooned. 'Strike a light!'

James said nothing. Then a little spark of anger suddenly made him say, 'Any fool could do those things quickly.'

'Who says we was trying to do them quickly?' the big boy answered.

19

'Thass right, Terry, you tell 'im!' piped up a long thin boy in a striped scarf.

'You'll get us all set more sums, you will,' a third boy said. 'An' if you do, bor, we'll murder yer!'

'Just moved here last week, and thinks he's village,' said Terry, shaking his head, and drawing languorously on his fag. 'Thass rich!'

'How long do you have to be here?' asked James.

'Born here,' a girl said. 'You can't move here and be village.'

'People must get born on that estate,' said James.

'But you wasn't,' said Terry, conclusively.

'Well, how long have *you* been here?' said James, returning Terry's stare. He was just a little more angry than dismayed.

'My family's always been here,' said Terry. 'I follow on.'

'So what about Angey?' James asked, seeing her standing apart a step or so, back to the fence, looking on.

'Angey stops in our playground,' said Terry. 'And don't you go picking on Angey, or I'll fix you good and proper. Right?'

'I'm not picking on her,' said James, 'I'm just asking, that's all.'

'Her great-gran come for the potato harvest in nineteen twenty-four,' said the boy with the scarf. 'Good enough?'

Once more the bell rescued James.

He came home by slipping down the tiny gravel path that led past the back doors of the terrace, and found his mother standing in the porch with a paint brush in her hand, talking to Gaffer Samson. The Gaffer had put down a scuttle of coal on the gravel, and was leaning on the gate.

'I'm whoolly middlin', thankee, m'm,' he said, as James arrived beside him.

James's mother looked baffled. 'Are you getting enough to eat, Mr Samson?' she asked.

'Can't fancy nothing,' he said. 'Never feels hungry no more. Meals on Wheels brings me dinners Sundays, and Patsy, that's me Home Help, gets a bit cooked for me her days, but I throw the most of it away.'

'You ought to eat,' said James's mother.

'Rather spend me money keeping warm,' Gaffer said. 'Oi do feel the cold. Now when my old lady was alive she used to make a lovely rice pudding, and I'd sup it up that fast she'd say I was Gaffer Gobbler; but that in tins isn't a patch on what hers was.'

'Well, no,' said James's mother. 'James will carry the coal for you, won't you, James?'

'He carted that for me t'other morning,' said Gaffer. 'Reckon he'll do that now. Him and me's good friends. Thass a good boy you've got, m'm.'

'Glad you think so, Mr Samson,' said James's mother, sounding mildly surprised.

James staggered into Gaffer Samson's porch, and past the heavy velveteen curtain across the door, into his living-room. His eye fell on a brown faded lady looking out of a photograph frame, and a huge number of medicine bottles on a table by the fireside chair, but he didn't want to stay; he put the coal down, and went back to his own house.

The living-room in his house had been transformed: old sheets had been cast over the furniture, and a coat of very pale yellow paint applied to the walls. It looked bright and inviting. James's mother was on the sitting-room floor, painting the skirting white.

'Can I do anything?' asked James, putting his school-bag down on the ghostly sheeted bulk of the settee.

'You with a paint brush?' his mother said. 'Ugh! No, thank you, son. Ask again later.'

James went upstairs to his attic. He looked out of all the windows. He sat down and considered where to hang his model plane. A bookcase had appeared in the room, and he unpacked a tea-chest of books into it. Then he went downstairs. He felt restless and pointless, as though he was somewhere he was just visiting, not somewhere he lived. His mother was in the kitchen now, weighing out ingredients.

'Butter those dishes for me, will you, James?' she said. A large and a small glass dish stood on the side. James began to smear them with butter.

'Let me guess,' he said. 'Rice pudding – well, well!'

'Where's the harm, James?' said his mother. 'What if it is? How was school?'

'All right,' said James.

'Homework?'

'None.'

'That's nice, then. Why don't you go for a walk?'

James went down to the river and looked at it. It wasn't a tumbling, athletic one like the river at home. It was wide and green and quiet, and so smooth only the rapid travel of a stray twig on its surface showed that it was moving, and in haste. There were trees beside it, and on the other bank a wide, wide green meadow stretched to a just discernible rise in the land. A path led along the river bank to the church. James plodded there and back, deep in gloom.

Later he took the little rice pudding down the row to Mr Samson.

'How are you liking here?' the Gaffer asked him. Just in time James stopped himself saying it was horrible, and remarked instead, 'It's flat.'

'That is flat hereabouts,' Gaffer said. 'I'll have that pudding for me dinner, thankee kindly.'

'Have you ever been in Yorkshire, Gaffer?' said James.

'Yuss. In the war. Had to go where you was sent.'

'Did you like the hills?'

'Cost a lot of sky, they do,' said the Gaffer. 'I like sky.'

'Oh,' said James. 'And you never wanted to go back?'

'Never had the money to go nowhere,' the Gaffer said. 'Long hours and low wages, thass what I had. Went on an outing to Great Yarmouth, once. I bin a cowman, and I bin a coalman. I laboured at this and that. Hadn't got much, couldn't get much. Never been so well off as I am on the pension.'

'And you don't mind being stuck here?'

'I wouldn't say stuck, bor. I'd say steady. God made the hills; that's his doing. But men made the fen. That has been forest and that has been sea, and now that's land to live on.'

'That's interesting to know, Gaffer,' said James, 'but not interesting to look at.'

'Some folks is picky,' said the Gaffer. 'Some folks is hard to please.'

When James's father asked him that evening, 'How are you getting on, son?', James said darkly, 'Whoolly middlin',' and made his mother stare.

'I'm stuck, Miss!' wailed Angey. 'Miss! Miss, I can't do these flippin' sums. Someone's gotta help me.'

'The best help you could have, Angela,' said Miss Dean, 'would be to come to school regularly, and give yourself a chance.'

'I can't help it if I keep getting flu,' said Angey.

'Really, Angela!' exclaimed Miss Dean. 'Do you really suppose, when you "have flu" sitting down by the river all day, or wandering all over the fields, that you suddenly become invisible, and nobody sees you, and tells the school? Truancy is the name of what you keep getting.'

'Well, I'm here today,' said Angey, sulkily, 'and I can't do these sums.'

'I'm not surprised,' said Miss Dean, tartly. 'And I'm busy at the moment doing something else. When you have attended school for a week without missing any days at all, so that I see you have begun to try, then I will help you.'

'James isn't busy,' said Angey. 'Can't he help me?'

James jumped at the sound of his own name. He had been looking out of the window; indeed, looking out of the window was how he spent most maths times. He was watching a toy tractor, crawling across the field, ploughing. It was shrunk to toy size by level distance, just as cars on the Skipton road had been by being seen from the fellside far above. It was ploughing, miles away; only a litter of gulls, tiny white specks flocking after it, could tell you that it was turning the earth . . .

'I'm sure James isn't the only one who has finished,' Miss Dean said. 'Who will help Angey? Can I have a volunteer?'

Not one hand went up. Miss Dean waited. James sighed. You could see things coming in this place. Out there on the fen you could have run all day, and still been in full view of what you were running away from! And in here James could see Angey coming; Angey's problems to wrestle with as well as his own. Not her maths problems; he expected to be able to do those. Her other problems. Angey couldn't so much as go into the estate children's playground. They were horrible to her. They called her names, and pointed to her grubby neck, and said she smelt; or at least they did if Terry wasn't anywhere near. In the village playground Angey was safe; Terry had said he would fix anyone who picked on her, and everyone believed him. But that didn't mean Terry was nice to her. Nobody was. She just stood by the fence, watching. Being Angey's friend would be like having a catching disease. James could see it would.

James was determined to manage to be village in the end. All the tough boys and all the interesting girls were village. And the village mob might have a weak spot in Peter, the boy with the scarf. He wore it so often they actually called him Scarf. Scarf was good at football, and good at cricket, James heard. And he was famous for having climbed up a high tree to rescue a cat. Terry had

been there too, but he was too solid and heavy for the job and Scarf had done it. James had been studying Scarf for some time, and he thought he could get under his guard. Scarf drew planes a lot. He might like model planes, too. And now here was Angey, being tied round James's neck.

Nobody volunteered to help her; Miss Dean sighed, and asked him. James plodded to the back of the class, sat down beside Angey, and looked at her book. She was miles and miles behind everybody else. He began to show her how to work long division. Within ten minutes James had learned two things about Angey: first she wasn't stupid at all, and probably didn't need the help she had asked for – she must just have been acting stupid to get her claws into him; and second that she did really truly smell, when you sat right beside her, though it wasn't a nasty smell, just earthy, like the vegetable rack in the shop. James couldn't think how he was ever going to escape her. He would have to be really mean to her to shake her off, and being mean to Angey would be a nasty thing to have to do, even if it escaped a terrible revenge from Terry.

He put his head round the back door when he got home, and called to his mother, 'Mum! I'm back. I'm just fetching some coal in for the Gaffer.'

His mother came down the stairs at once. 'James! James, dear, I've got bad news for you. Mr Samson isn't here, he's in hospital. He fell off his bike and hurt himself.'

'O.K.,' said James. 'Then I don't have to heave his coal around the place. Good.' He plodded up the stairs. But he felt bad. The empty house next door felt like a gap in a row of teeth. A bad day. A bad day altogether.

'Well,' said James's father, folding the paper swiftly and patting it as it lay beside his plate. 'Here's the first fine Saturday since we got here. Where shall we go?'

'There's an awful lot to do in the house,' said James's mother. 'What about putting down the stair carpet?'

'That's for the first rainy Saturday,' Father said. 'Where do you want to go?'

'What about Ely?' Mother said. 'I'd love to go to Ely! You two wash up, and I'll just fix a picnic.'

'No, love, no more freezing March picnics. We are going to find a nice restaurant and eat in the warm and dry.'

'What's Ely?' asked James.

'Cathedral. Not a boring one.'

'Mum? Mum, could we go and see Gaffer Samson? Is his hospital on the way?'

'Hmph,' said Mother. 'It's not on the way, I'm afraid. But we could, James. It gets dark quite early still, so we will have to be through sightseeing by visiting time; we could go a long way round coming back.'

'You amaze me,' said James's father. 'I'm not criticizing, James, just curious. But whatever do you want to visit Mr Samson for? You've only known him a few weeks, and you can't have much in common with the poor old boy.'

'I like his voice,' said James. 'He sounds full of gravel when he talks. He says "Orr, borr, dew yew put it tharr, thass roight …"'

Both his parents laughed. 'James, dear,' said his mother, 'he's very old, you know. Poor old man, and he hurt himself quite badly, I think. It might be a bit upsetting, going to see him.'

'I think he likes me, Mum,' said James. 'And he's the only person in this whole place who does. He's the only one who has said one nice thing to me so far. Well, except for Angey,' he added, reluctantly truthful.

'Is it being a bit tough making new friends, old son?' said his father. 'Often is, at first.'

'The thing is,' said James, recklessly, 'they're all either village or estate, and they don't reckon I'm either. Everyone is one or the other except me and Angey.'

'Shall we see if Angey is free to come with us today?' said Mother brightly. 'Would that be nice?'

'That would be *horrible*!' yelled James. 'Angey is just *awful*! And I have to keep helping her with her sums!'

James's parents looked at each other, meaningfully. They said not a word, and their silence spoke worlds of warning to James. He had really put his foot in it now.

'O.K., James,' his father said. 'We'll go to the hospital on the way home, if you really want to. Cheer up.'

'I'll try,' said James. 'Things keep cheering me down, that's all.'

They didn't go straight to Ely. James's parents weren't very good at going straight anywhere. They drove, and turned down side roads on impulse just to see if there was anything nice down them, and parked on grass verges, and got out and walked, and pointed their binoculars at birds, and talked furiously, and put dates to all the bits of all the churches, and called houses things like 'cruck-built' and 'pargetted' and 'local wilds'. James listened in the way he listened to the music they played on the car stereo; he let it flow over him, a familiar flood of sound, to which you didn't pay any real attention, so that all the details escaped you but the flavour reached you. James's parents were excited, being on new ground. They always liked covering new ground.

James just sat in the back seat, and looked. They were driving at one point on a road that was just a foot or two higher than the fields on either side. Two ditches full of water ran beside it left and right all the way. Then they were on a road running half way up a steep green bank. Father parked, and they all got out and climbed to the top of the bank, to look what it was. A wide river was running in the top of the bank, not brimming, but at a level much higher than the land below. Below them long straight ditches full of water ran into another drain, that followed the foot of the river bank, below the road.

'I've read about this,' Father said. 'The land shrank when they drained it, so the original dykes are left stranded, high up. They have to pump the water up into the rivers – yes, look – that building on the bank ahead of us must be a pumping station. Shall we walk along and look?'

But standing on top of the river bank they were being buffeted by a strong cold wind that reached their skin through their coats, as though it had been ice-cold water, and their bones through their skins, as though they had been standing in it for hours instead of just minutes. The strength and speed and chill of it coming off the huge expanse of sodden land below took your breath away.

'It's just a touch too bracing for walking,' said Mother, and they all scrambled down the grassy slope, back to the car.

James stood, shoulders hunched to lift the collar of his duffle coat high around his ears, waiting for the back door of the car to be unlocked. On the black field a flickering black and white throng of birds hopped and flew, skimming the soil. Half the vastness was black, ploughed, the other half bright green with tiny blades of winter wheat. No hedge divided crop from crop.

'Why aren't there any trees?' James asked, shutting himself gratefully into the warmth of the car.

'The water table is too high, I think,' Father said. 'The

whole thing would be marsh, or deep lakes if it wasn't drained.'

'The Gaffer said that,' James murmured, but his mother wasn't listening.

'Lapwings!' she said. 'Look at the lapwings, James. And I think that's Ely, over there.'

'It's twenty miles to Ely,' Father said, driving off.

'Just the same, I think that's it; that grey thing breaking the skyline . . .'

James thought she couldn't be right, really. Everything here shrank; a tractor in the next field looked like a toy; a person moving like an ant. The distance overpowered everything, and made it seem a speck of no importance; nothing twenty miles away, or even five miles away, could be big enough to stand and be seen.

But his mother was right. The grey jutting speck on the skyline was Ely. Someone had seen what to do. Someone crawling, or drowning, in this vastness had answered flatness with height, and distance with huge size. Someone had built a hill out of grey stone, an immense, intricate, hollow, holy mountain, and topped it with an enormous lantern: someone had built something that would not shrink out of sight while still in your line of vision, even from far, far, across the shrinking and inhuman fen.

James liked it, a lot. He liked it inside and outside, but specially outside, and he bought himself six postcards of it, all different, standing up complicated from the simple flatness of the land.

★

Father waited for them in Reception. James and his mother went up three flights of green and white staircase, and along a corridor to a ward. There were curtains round the Gaffer's bed, but visits were allowed. You had to ask the ward sister first, though. She told James's mother that Gaffer had been wandering. 'I tried to make it out,' she said. 'We always try; sometimes it does mean something or another ... but he was far gone. He was asking for something, very worked up wanting it, but when we said was it lost, he said no, if it was lost he wouldn't be here, but he wanted it back! Dear, oh dear. But he's better today, I think. Making sense. I'm glad to see you; he hasn't had a visitor. His family is just a sister, I gather, and she's pushing ninety, and poorly.'

The Gaffer was a funny greenish colour against a very white pillow. 'What you want to bother with me for?' he said. 'Got nothing to do, haven't you?'

'We've been to Ely,' said James. 'I'm sorry you fell off your bike.'

'I never fell without I was pushed,' he said. 'Been riding a bike more'n eighty years, and never fell off afore.'

'Pushed, Mr Samson? Did something hit you?' said Mother.

'Farm lorry come past me so fast that gusted and blew me off,' he said.

'Ah,' said Mother.

'Makes you think every minute will be your next,' he added. 'What's the world coming to? That's the end of boiking, mind. I'm all wore out; can't ride no more. The boy had better have the bike, m'm. That'll take him about a bit. Shed's not locked, bor. Do you have the bike.'

'Thank you, Gaffer,' said James. 'When are you coming home?'

'Don't know that, bor. They gives us a chance to die here. Them as don't make it gets sent home to do it. They'll send me home, by and by.'

'Things aren't so bad, then, Mr Samson,' said Mother, anxiously.

'Roll on Christmas, let's have some nuts!' he said, grinning suddenly.

Mother made James come away. 'We mustn't get him tired,' she said. But she stopped at the ward office, and spoke to the sister in a low voice. James waited, fidgeting, overhearing most of it. The nurse's whisper had a good deal of carrying power. 'Won't be long . . .' James heard. 'Riddled with it, Mrs Lang, just riddled with it . . . miracle he's still here . . . must have been in pain . . . never complained . . . never seen a doctor . . . only a few weeks at most . . . doing all we can . . . had a good run for his money . . . yes, I'm afraid so . . .'

Mother came out looking serious, and led James back through corridors and stairs to Father reading a coverless magazine in Reception. It was dark outside, now. Dark when they got home.

A thing about the banister rail, and the stair to James's room, with no door, was that he could hear more than he used to be able to when he was lying in bed. In the Yorkshire house he had to get up, and crouch on the landing to hear anything much; here he could be lying in his own bed, breaking no rules at all, and still catch voices.

'It seems they will send him out, even with nobody to look after him,' he heard his mother say.

'Unless he dies first,' said Father.

'He seems to have got it into his head that he won't be able to, that they'll have to send him home,' said Mother. 'He ought to be wrong, according to medical science, but it's mind over matter again. He gave James his bike, Peter. Do you see any objection?'

'I'd better check it first, if it's been in an accident. More coffee for you?' His father got up to make coffee, and closed the door, and James's innocent overhearing stopped short.

The bike was black, heavy and battered. The saddle and handlebars had rusted solidly in place at a point far too high for James, and Father had to use penetrating oil to free them and lower them. But everything worked, the chain was oiled, the brake pads were nearly new. Father grunted, and, James could see, rethought Gaffer Samson as he checked. At last he said, 'O.K., son, she's all yours,' and James pedalled off, slithering on the gravel path, and gaining sudden steadiness and speed on the tarmac, and raced away down the road, rejoicing. He sped past the school and turned down a narrow path between walls, riding over the bumpy ruts and sludgy dips in the path, and weaving a neat slalom between the stile-posts, and so on, on, to another road and into a field and down the riverside footpath where a council notice said clearly NO CYCLING, and past a house between the village and the next, where a dog ran out and barked and ran with him, and so round by the main road, home again breathless and dizzy with speed, his head singing with the hiss of the tyres on the road and the plucking, guitar-string sound of freewheeling, and his legs aching at the back of his knees.

There were five roads leading out of the village, and each one led to another village within a level several miles; two roads were winding, three were straight as rulers, all were easy riding, and James rode them all and back again, learning the names of the churches he had seen on the skyline; that spire was Bluntisham, and that one Fenstanton, and that tower was Over, or Cottenham, and once you knew down which road the village lay, and what shape its church was, you could steer yourself by churches across the vast featureless land, like stars for a mariner at sea. The land remembered being water; it was soaked in ultra-violet, all its distances purple, as though it was the sea, and the boisterous wind buffeted James as he went, so that his bike leaned and straightened, and rocked the rider like a boat on waves, and he struggled like a sailor fighting to hold the tiller. And the villages were like harbours, their snuggling houses standing shoulder to shoulder against the wind's force, so that as James rode in there was a sudden peace and smooth going, breakwind instead of breakwater.

After the fifth village, James rode home and slept. He could not climb to bed aloft, his knees hurt so; he just lay on the bottom stairs and slept, and slept.

His parents climbed over him for an hour or two, before waking him and chivvying him to bed with a mug of chocolate instead of supper.

The Monday afternoon after Ely the tractor stopped. It was ploughing much nearer the school, in the middle distance from the classroom window, and half way through the afternoon nature lesson it just stopped. Then in a little while another tractor arrived, a yellow one beside the red one, and a crowd of men gathered, standing around. James was not the only one looking; the class stirred, turned heads, whispered. Miss Dean rapped on the desk, and tried to make them think about the tadpoles on the poster she had hung up for them, but heads still turned, eyes flicked to the scene outside, and back to the poster again. Then the Headmistress came into the room, and spoke briefly to Miss Dean in an undertone. Miss Dean said, 'Stand up, everyone. Coats on, and outdoor shoes, please, as quick as you can. There is something for us to see. Quietly now!'

It felt strange to James to be plodding across the field instead of looking at it framed in the classroom window; as though he had been watching something on television, and suddenly found himself acting in it. It was much further across the field than he expected; they were walking in single file, between rows of green soft blades, and soft black earth stuck to their boots and shoes. Even in single file the others were all talking happily together, pretending to grumble. 'Me Dad'll be hopping mad when I tell 'im,' Terry was saying. 'He don't send me to school for traipsing, but for learning sums.'

At last they crossed from the field of winter wheat to the field that was being ploughed, and came up to the group of men. They were digging. They had dug out a huge tree stump, and, beside it, the end of the fallen trunk. It was a black, whale-backed thing, rising just above the surface of the field, as though it were floating, waterlogged, in the black earth. The plough had snagged on it, and broken a share-blade. The men had got a length of chain wound round the end of the trunk, and hooked on to the red tractor's towing-bar. Miss Dean made them stand well clear.

'Whass the world coming to?' said the farmer, grinning at her. 'When I was in your class we wasn't took about sightseeing. All hard graft, thenadays!'

'Rubbish, Bob,' said Miss Dean. 'I distinctly remember you on a botany picnic at Wicken Fen.'

'When I fell in the dyke,' he said. 'Ah. Well, this'll be something to see.'

The driver put the tractor into gear, and the chain tightened, but nothing happened. The huge tyres began to spin, and bite grooves in the ground. The farmer called out to the driver, who stopped. They brought up some wire fence panels, and laid them out under the wheels of the tractor, and then they backed the second tractor alongside, and put a length of chain from the tree to that one too. Then they tried again. And behind the snorting, roaring machines a long, long line of black earth heaved up; the ground shuddered, and up came the tree trunk, very slowly at first, and then as it freed itself from the weight and cling of the earth, faster, and then a huge, thick length of black timber was trundling away across the neatly ridged furrows, leaving a flattened wake behind it, to be dumped in the grassy verge of the nearest dyke.

Everyone walked along behind to look at it.

'Thass big, that is,' the driver of the yellow tractor remarked.

'Biggest I've seen,' said the farmer. 'Good riddance.'

'What will you do with it?' asked Scarf.

'Nothing. Nothing to be done with that. When that's wet through like now, that's all soft and stringy, and the saw won't cut; and when that dries out, that gets all cracked and hard as iron, and you still can't cut the beggar. That'll leave lying just where that is.'

'How long is it?' asked Tracy.

'Can we measure it?' said Miss Dean, at once.

They all paced the length of it, to and fro. Ninety feet. It was ninety feet.

'We should tell the *Echo*, Bill,' said one of the men. 'Thass a record, should be. Must have been a fine old forest when that was standing up.'

'A forest? Right here?' said James.

'That's a forest tree, see,' said the farmer, 'because it goes all the way without branches. No big boles on the trunk for where there was branches. If they have space around them, they grow branches; this one had to go up

ninety feet for light. Bad news, that is; I'll find a few more in the field next year.'

James tipped his head back, and tried to imagine ninety feet high into the empty sky. He was pleasantly astonished at the thought of fallen forest lying lurking underground in this treeless place. But his cheerful mood did not last long. When they got back into the school building his mother was waiting to see Miss Dean.

At first James was just waiting. Everyone else rushed about, collecting schoolbags, grabbing books, going home. James in his duffle coat sat at his desk, gloomily waiting. He ought to have known better than to have told his mother about school. Angey was hanging around, too.

'Coming?' she asked, from the classroom door.

'Got to wait,' he said, scowling. The racket of children flowed out of the school building, and ebbed across the playground towards the gate. Behind it came a hush, seeping through the rooms. It wasn't natural, being alone in school. Then James realized that in the freshly flowing silence he could hear a hum of voices, and then that he could distinguish every word.

He sighed, and kicked the floor. This was the least private place he had ever been in. You could see everything, and hear everything. James sat and thought about hills, and standing trees, and doors that shut and made places with edges ... no use. He could hear his mother complaining bitterly about his being held back at maths, instead of being 'brought on' with extra work. She was also demanding that what went on in the playground was kept a firm eye on; James was appalled. He wanted to drop through a hole in the scuffed parquet floor. But a little flicker of joy somewhere inside him lit up at the knowledge that his mother was angry; that she was so fiercely on his side.

Then suddenly he saw that Angey was still there, just outside the classroom door, listening too. His eyes met hers. 'Your mum's triffic!' she murmured, and then shot out of sight at his furious *'Go away!'*

'Do try to understand the situation,' came Miss Dean's voice. She meant to be speaking quietly, but teachers lose the knack. 'It really is very hard on the real children, to be constantly faced with incomers, always brighter than them, always outsmarting them, always top of the class . . .'

'James is a real child!' said Mother, loud and clear, and, oh!, thought James, so angry!

'Course he is,' said Angey's voice from just outside the door.

'James!' his mother yelled. He walked reluctantly to the door, to see his mother bearing down on him along the corridor, with two bright red patches of rage on her cheeks.

'In the car!' she said, sweeping towards the door. 'Is this Angey? Get in, Angey, you're coming too!'

The car shot out of the school gates, and swung alarmingly fast round the roundabout; then it turned on to the dual-carriageway, and roared up to seventy. They were in Cambridge in no time at all, and lurched suddenly into a parking space just as a car vacated it. Down King's Parade Mother marched them, Angey hopping and running along behind them, and into the warm glow of the

Copper Kettle. James thought he saw the waitress raise an eyebrow at Angey, but Mother stared her down. They settled at a little corner table, and scanned a copy of the huge menu.

'Anything you like,' said Mother.

'Even if it might spoil my supper?' said James, trying to size up the opportunity.

'This is your supper,' Mother said. 'Feel free. I'm going to have ham sandwiches, and scones and cream, and a choice of cakes.'

James ate a lot. He was feeling very sore, and eating helped. Mother ate a lot, and calmed down slowly as she filled up. But Angey ate as though it were the first and last meal of her life; on and on and on, in no sort of order, asking for chicken sandwiches after jam, scones and cake, and getting them.

'Should I phone your mother and tell her where you are, Angey?' Mother said when they found themselves outside again in a soft blue dusk. 'Will she be worried?'

'Me gran,' said Angey. 'No, she won't be back long herself. We haven't got no phone.'

'What about your mother?' persisted James's mother.

'Went off two year ago,' said Angey. 'Thanks ever so much for the tea, Missus. It do make you feel good!'

'I feel sick,' said James.

'You must have eaten too much then, boy,' said Mother crisply.

'I didn't eat half as much as Angey!' said James indignantly.

'No rude comments, James,' said Mother unlocking the car door for them.

They went home much more slowly, and round by the trailer park, to leave Angey. The trailer park had roads, and little gardens round the vans; they were so parked they looked like houses. Angey's was right at the back, beside the river. It looked shabbier than most, and had only rough grass round it instead of garden. There was no light on in it. Mother sat in the car and watched as Angey pulled a key on a string from under her anorak, and let herself in.

'You'll have to snap out of feeling sick, James,' she said, driving slowly between the rows of vans. 'They brought Mr Samson home this morning, and put him to bed in his sitting-room, and he's asking to see you.'

'I'm not really feeling sick,' James said, 'I'm feeling sorry.' But his mother didn't guess he meant sorry he had ever said a word about things at school.

'I'm sorry too, James,' she said. 'Poor old fellow. It doesn't seem right, when all he wants is to slip away quietly, and he can't manage it. And he shouldn't be alone, even with Home Helps and district nurses coming in and out. He did ask specially for you, son. I think you should go in for a minute or two.'

'Yes,' said James, 'I'll go in as soon as we get home if there isn't going to be any supper.'

The Gaffer was lying propped up on a mountain of pillows, facing the television set across the room. A boxing match was on, making intermittent bursts of noise, against a hysterically chattering and shrieking voice. The Gaffer's eyes were shut.

'Hullo,' said James. 'Are you feeling better?'

'Whoolly middlin',' said the Gaffer, opening his eyes. 'Ah, that's you, bor. Sit down.'

James sat in the bulging armchair across the fireside from the bed. 'Did you want me to bring coal, Gaffer?' he asked.

'Twasn't that,' the Gaffer said. His breathing was getting a bit in the way of his sentences. 'Boike all right?'

'The bike's terrific!' said James. 'I went to Fenstanton, and Bluntisham, and Cottenham and . . .'

'Thought you didn't like it much, herearound,' said the Gaffer.

'It's good for biking,' said James.

'Want you to get something for me,' said the Gaffer. 'If you'd be so kind.'

'What is it?' said James.

'My luck. I need that back now. And I can't go nowhere no more. I was set out to get that when I come off me boike and into hospital. Never thought of being laid up when I put that safe hid. And you'm me only chance, bor. They all think I'm gone twisty when I ask for it, like. There's only you I *can* ask.'

'Where is it?'

'Underneath the loose stone in the hearth in the cottage I lived in time gone by.'

'Who lives there now?' said James, apprehensively, not liking the idea of having to talk his way in.

'No one. That's mostly fallen down.'

'O.K. What is it, exactly, I'm to look for?'

'That's a little leaf of stone, wrapped in a flour bag. My luck.'

'Will it make you better if I find it?'

'Nothing of the sort, bor. Nothing like. But I do need it mainly.'

'A piece of luck,' said James, thinking. 'But not to make you better.'

'No. I'll tell you about that, when I can get me breath to it. Long ago. I'm your age, see. Well, a bit older then. I'm fourteen. And I'm walking along the field edge with a rabbit, that I took in a trap. I was good at trappin' rabbits. That's a bright day with a proud sky full of clouds. Corn is ripe. Corn is gold with the poppies shouting red. And there's a young mauther coming towards me in a red dress; a nut-brown mauther with a red dress torn off one shoulder, and her's singing like a bird as she come.'

'What's a *mauther*, for heaven's sake?' asked James.

'A young woman to you. A bit of a girl. And she says, "Give us the rabbit, bor. The little ones is hungry." So I give it her. Well, wass a rabbit to me? I know where there's more on 'em, and how to catch them. So then she reaches down in her dress enough to make me dizzy, and she bring out the piece of luck, still warm that was for all of its black black stone, and she give that to me, and she tell me about that. "Do you lose this," she tell me, "and you'll be dead afore the season changes. Do you give it away, and you'll take your chances like another man; but do you keep it, and there'll come no harm to you on land or water, your life long. Thass worth a rabbit," she says. So after I took the luck, I was frighted, then. Didn't want to lose that, whatever else. So I wrapped that up in one of my mother's flour bags, and I put that below the loose stone on the hearth, and it's been

45

seventy year, and no harm's come to me, good times or bad. And now's the time to get that back, and I can't move an inch no more than a mile.'

'That's all right,' said James. 'I'll get it for you. Is it far?'

'Two mile. Easy on a bike.'

'It's dark now,' said James. 'I'll come and see you in the morning, and you can give me directions.'

But the Gaffer didn't answer. James looked hard at him, and saw that he had fallen asleep.

'Out! And-he's-out-for-the-count!' screamed the television set. James got up quietly and switched the set off.

'I was watching that,' said the Gaffer, but before James could switch it on again, he was nodding, eyelids drooping.

James pushed aside the heavy velveteen curtain that hung across the door, and stepped through the always-unlocked back door to the outside path.

He stood for a moment outside looking at the starry sky. He must ask his mother some time if she believed in luck, and mascots and charms and suchlike. He thought somehow the answer would be no.

The directions were clear and easy sounding. The Gaffer's cottage had been down on the fen. You started at the Post Office in the High Street, and went down the path at the side of it, over the dyke and up a bit to the mill; from there right, down a bit, and when you got to the fen bank you could see it ahead. James got on the bike, and went off, cheerful.

Half way down the High Street he met Scarf.

'I'm looking for you,' said Scarf.

James wobbled a bit, and stood, astride the bike.

'You didn't oughter go riding that bike around all over the place,' said Scarf.

'Why not?' said James. 'What are bikes for?'

'You been seen,' said Scarf; and then: 'Terry seen you.'

'So?' said James.

'Estate kids stay on the estate, or just go to the shops,' said Scarf. 'They don't go belting round the lanes on bikes. Their mums don't let them.'

'So?' said James, wearily.

'Terry reckons you oughter stay in the village, and leave the lanes to us. Where'd you get the bike from, anyway? That's not new.'

'Gaffer gave it to me.'

Scarf whistled. 'Did he do? Terry reckons Gaffer Samson is his family. Why didn't he give it to Terry?'

'I've never seen Terry coming to see him!' said James.

'That's the trouble with you,' said Scarf thoughtfully. 'You oughter pipe down like everyone else, and you pipes up with answers. Look for trouble, you do.'

'No, I don't,' said James. 'I just get it. Why were you looking for me?'

'To tell you to watch yourself. Terry's on the warpath, what with your mum going up the school. I told him people can't help their mums, but he don't see it that way. Don't you go riding around all over the place, or he'll catch you. And don't tell anyone I told you, right? I'm off afore I get spotted talking to you.'

'Terrific,' said James. 'Bloody terrific.'

He did consider going home, and putting the bike in the shed for a while till Terry got something else on his mind, but that would be mean. It would really be mean not to do something for the Gaffer just because of Terry. He rode down to the Post Office. An old lady in a fur coat was just posting something through the letter-box fixed to the wall.

James stopped and stared. The Post Office was long, low and thatched. On one side it was joined on to a large dignified house, and the other side it was joined on to a funny little brick building shaped like a chapel, and called 'The Reading Rooms'.

There wasn't a path at the side of it at all.

James leaned on the bike and thought. There couldn't ever have been a path; the Post Office and the buildings each side of it had been built joined on, and must always have touched. And they looked pretty ancient. He trotted up and down the High Street some way each side of them, and he couldn't find a gap where a path was, or might have been. But if there had been a path, going somewhere from the High Street, it must have gone through to Church Lane, behind the High Street. James rode round into Church Lane, and looked for a path there.

He found one, running between two high brick walls. He rode along it. It emerged from between the walls, and ran along a field edge, beside some large modern houses with elaborately planted gardens. Then it joined a narrow road with overgrown banks and tall hedges. James rode down the road. The bike freewheeled; you couldn't see a slope, but the bike could feel it. The road was going down, not up a bit. At the end of the road was an old house, standing well back. A sign said MILL HOUSE. A wooden stile beside the garden railings was signposted RIGHT OF WAY. James heaved his bike over the stile, and followed RIGHT OF WAY, though it was probably wrong of way, because he had turned right down it, not left. It led almost at once to the river bank. A grey-painted lock superstructure stood across the river, and a waterfall sound of a weir came from behind hedges in the direction of the Mill House gardens. There wasn't any dyke to cross, or any fen bank in sight.

James went back to the road, and cycled towards the village back the way he had come, till he found a turning, on the left as you left the village, and tried that one. He was leaving the Mill House behind him; did a mill always stand right beside a house? He wondered about that for half a mile; then he was riding on a straight narrow road, with a ditch full of water on each side, between vast flat fields. Ahead to the right a church tower, very far off and small. Ahead to the left a church spire emerging from trees. The spire pointed at a tiny pale flake of gold, where the weathercock caught the afternoon sun. A vast sky overhead; a vast land all around, and everything that could be seen in any direction crowded into the narrow ribbon running round the rim of the land, where it met the curving down of the sky. It made James dizzy; the landmarks danced in space as he rode. The spire stood now on the right of the tower. And from the corner of his eye he caught movement far over on his right. Miles and miles away, riding on another road parallel to his own, he saw a group of cyclists, going east, with him. Even without seeing the pale blue speck of Terry's anorak, he would have known they were the village, chasing him. He put his head down, and pedalled furiously. The bike went at an amazing speed; but all the time, along the other road the other bikes kept up with him, no nearer, and no further, but full in view.

There was a turning on the road, a T-junction, with a signpost, going to the southern horizon, and taking him away from the pursuit. James turned down it, and pedalled with a lifting heart. Somewhere along it he would find a turning towards home; and they were stuck on their road, going in the old direction. He laughed. Then he saw them, still going, riding now along some road on his left, some road that must have turned from theirs as

his had turned from his. They were closer than before, riding fast, perhaps some half a mile away, and obviously riding a route that would cut across the land between him and home.

Black panic overtook him. Wherever he rode they would be able to see him; for miles and miles there was no cover, no tree or wood, only flat and naked earth. And they knew all the roads. They would catch him soon. He nearly ran into the back of a bus which had parked beside the narrow verge, although it had hazard lights flashing, for he was frightened out of even the sense to look where he was going.

James skidded, the bike slewed on the gravel chip-

pings, and he saved himself with difficulty. People were getting off the bus, grumbling, and one of the people, weighed down with bulging shopping bags, and a parcel under each arm, was Miss Dean. James wheeled his bicycle up to her.

'Whatever are you doing, out here, James?' she said.

'Just riding,' he said. 'Can I help you with those things?'

'Well, I don't know *what* to do,' she said. 'I think these things are too heavy for you to carry, James, and too heavy for me too. I was expecting to get off at the bus stop in the village, right by my own front door, and now the bus has broken down, and we have a mile to walk home. Dear, oh dear. Perhaps I can leave things on the bus, and claim them later.'

'You carry one of the parcels,' said James, 'and one will go in the handlebar basket, and the bags will go one on each handlebar, and I will wheel the bike.'

'Could you really?' she said. 'How very kind of you, James. I will accept your offer.'

The bike was heavy and wobbly to wheel with all Miss Dean's shopping on it, but James didn't mind. They began to walk straight towards Terry and his friends, the shortest way home. Miss Dean told James that the very heavy bag, which kept tugging the handlebars to the right, had books in it from shops in Cambridge, books about the fen.

'Are there books about it?' asked James. He remembered books about Yorkshire that his grandad had, full of shiny colour photographs of Micklegate Bar, and of York Minster, and the Dales, and Moors and seacoast . . . 'What is there to say?'

'Well, I got one about Bog Oaks, and Buried Forests,' said Miss Dean. 'I was so interested in that tree we saw the other day. And one about the draining of Whittlesea Mere — that's the last bit that was under water and marshy. And one with a chapter about Fen Fires. So you see, there is quite a lot to write about.'

'What's a fen fire?' said James. 'What is there to burn?'

'The ground itself burns, if farmers are careless burning stubble, or making bonfires. And once lit it will burn the earth for years, under the surface, and it's very hard to put out.'

'Someone told me about that,' said James, 'but I didn't believe it, really. It's all so wet and soggy!'

'I know. Isn't it interesting? You can borrow the book if you like when I have finished with it, though you might find it a bit hard. It isn't a children's book.'

'I'd like to look at it,' said James.

'That's nice,' said Miss Dean. 'I shan't feel so extravagant buying it, if other people read it too. And I know Mr Francis will like to borrow it. You won't know Mr Francis, James, being so new, but he used to keep the Post Office for many years, till it got too much for him. It used to take hours to buy a stamp, he talked so much, and he got worse as he got older, but I miss talking to him, every time I need to post a letter! The new people are very efficient, of course, and there is lots more room in the new Post Office ...'

'A new Post Office?' said James. 'You mean the Post Office hasn't always been where it is now?'

'No, only since last year sometime. Mr Francis didn't want to move, and that other cottage was for sale, and the Parish Council didn't mind them putting in a shop window, so Mr Francis stayed put, and the Post Office moved.'

'Is there a path beside his house?' asked James. But suddenly there appeared in front of them the village, led by Terry, rounding a turn from a joining track, and near enough to recognize Miss Dean. They came to a sudden stop, lined up across the road.

'Goodness!' said Miss Dean, 'what a lot of my class are out riding this afternoon!'

Terry gave James one blood-freezing scowl, and began to turn his bike, but Miss Dean called him back. 'Come on, Terry, you surely aren't going to let little James trolley all these heavy things. How about some help?'

So Scarf got one shopping bag, and Terry got another, and Janice got the parcel Miss Dean had been carrying, and they all walked together the last half mile into the village while Miss Dean kept up a one-sided cheerful conversation as far as her front door.

Her house was in the High Street, overlooked on all sides by windows: little sideways sashes, and new double-glazed Georgian panes, and a cast-iron Gothic with a dozen points, and wide serene Victorian bays, and most with net curtains behind them, so that you couldn't, from the street, see if anyone was looking out at you or not, but the net twitched now and then, to tell you they often were. James was safe in the High Street. He even risked a smile at Scarf, before detaching himself from the group, and making a smart retreat for home.

'Moved the Post Office?' said the Gaffer. 'I haven't

been in for my pension much recently. Mrs Marshal gets it for me, and a stamp for writing to my sister when I wants. Moved it, you say?'

'If you could just tell me where it used to be, I could find the path tomorrow,' said James.

'Changing things all the time,' the Gaffer said. 'Can't leave nothing alone, they can't. What I've seen, since thenadays! All changes, all for the wuss. Most disbugger-able!'

'But where was it?'

'That was under the hearthstone, down home, bor, where I said.'

'The Post Office,' James persisted. 'Where was it before it moved?'

'Down the High Street this side, and fourth house on the left,' said the Gaffer.

'O.K.,' said James. 'Thanks. Leave it to me.'

'Don't be no longer than you can help, bor,' said the Gaffer. 'I'm starting to hurt.'

James counted houses, one, two, three, four – he might have known! At the fourth house a long solid wall began and ran some distance along the High Street. It joined house to house, and was broken only by a gateway into a new house with a garage drive. There was no path.

'Oh, heck!' said James, and stamped in fury.

'Whass the matter, James?' said Angey, appearing from nowhere.

'It's you,' he remarked, gloomily.

'I always am,' she said, grinning. 'What's up?'

'I'm trying to do an errand for a crazy old man,' said James, crossly, 'and I can't make head or tail of his directions! There's supposed to be a path here, by the fourth house.'

'The path is further along. Come and I'll show you.'

'I've been on the wrong path before. It is supposed to be by the fourth house. But he's off his rocker, really. He didn't even know where the Post Office is.'

'Well, if he didn't remember about the Post Office, perhaps he's only counting the old houses,' said Angey. 'Most of these are new.'

'Are they?' said James. They didn't look new; they had gardens round them, not building site. They looked very settled and pleased.

'They was building them my first year at school,' said Angey. 'Let's try counting to four, counting only the old ones.'

It was a good idea, James could see. Angey might be awful, but she was sharp.

'O.K.,' he said.

The first house was made of heavy timbers, and pink-washed walls. That was not just old, it was positively medieval. Next to it was a long drive leading to a bungalow, set well back.

'Bungalows aren't old,' said James.

'That one isn't,' said Angey, 'anyway. So we're counting one.'

Next came a row of three, square, solid, box-shaped houses.

'Them's all new,' said Angey.

'No, they're not,' said James. He couldn't imagine his

parents saying cruck-built, or pargetted or whatever about those, but they looked worn, old-fashioned.

'Not to us, but to Mr Samson they are, bet you,' said Angey.

James had not told her it was for Gaffer Samson he was running an errand, but he wasn't surprised she knew. They plodded further, James wheeling his bike, and came to a large yellow-brick house with a pair of huge cedar trees in the garden, towering above the red-ridged roof.

'Two,' they said, both together. Next to that came a funny little house, facing its gable end on to the street, that wasn't quite straight on any of its corners, and that had a wide, wide, front door, pushed slightly out of true. 'Three,' said James, making sure he got it out first.

Then came a row of brick houses, with bright squared windows, and tiny fenced gardens, and garages where the front-room window might have been. 'None of those,' said James.

'Still three,' said Angey.

And then came an old wall, an old stile, and a sign pointing down a path, saying PUBLIC FOOTPATH.

'This is the path,' said Angey.

'But we've only got to three houses, and it's supposed to be beside four,' said James. Beyond the path was another large brick house with curling gables, obviously old; he went beyond it again looking for another path, but there wasn't one.

'No, hang about,' said Angey. 'Look, we didn't count those new houses with garages . . .'

'They're too new,' said James.

'But what about before they was built? Perhaps there

was a house pulled down to make room for them, and that makes it add up to four?'

'How would we find out?' asked James, once again impressed by Angey's grip.

'We could go down this path and see, turnip-top!' she said.

James paused. He weighed up the risks. The path was walled on both sides for some way, and then he could see the green light of the open fields. He couldn't expect Miss Dean to turn up in the middle of nowhere two days running.

'It's all right,' Angey said. 'Terry's mum took him into Huntingdon this morning to get his hair cut. We got till the afternoon bus at four o'clock.'

'*We?*' said James. 'Terry isn't after you, is he? He sticks up for you.'

'Just because he looks after me doesn't mean I gotta like him,' she said. 'Are we going down this path or ain't we?'

They went down it, in a tunnel of shade, under trees and between walls, and out into a blaze of sunshine on open country. There was a wide field, very gently rising to a low skyline.

'Rape,' said Angey.

'*What?*' said James. 'What did you say?'

'Rape. Oilseed rape. That's what's growing, thick-head.'

'Oh,' said James.

'Grows so yeller in May it hurts your eyes,' she said. 'Gotta wear sunglasses. Honest.'

'Give over,' said James. His bike was getting hard to push, picking up mud on the tyre treads, pulling sticky and heavy. He laid it down on the narrow verge, and went on without it. But it was obvious they were lost; there wasn't really a path, just field. What had Gaffer said? 'Over the dyke, and up a bit to the mill . . .'

'We should have crossed a dyke, Angey,' he said.

'Back a bit then,' she said.

Where the path came out from between the walls there was a ditch full of water, and a little wooden bridge,

barely more than a plank and a rail laid across it. Beyond was a proper path, going between hedges, and wide enough for a cart. It mounted a gentle rise. James cheered up a bit; this looked right, and you could follow it without the entire neighbourhood to a distance of thirty miles knowing what you were doing and exactly where you were. They trudged on. The path reached a low and gentle crest, opened out into a small space between hedges, and stopped.

'It's supposed to go to a mill,' said James.

'Well, it doesn't,' said Angey.

James looked all around, hoping to see something – a round brick tower like the derelict one beside the school, or a house, like the Mill House in the village. But there was nothing, and even the modest height on which they stood gave them enormous scope for seeing things, if they were there to be seen.

'To the mill, and then down a bit,' said James, sighing.

'You could go down three or four ways from here,' said Angey, and, indeed, you could; three little trails led along the field sides, and the land sloped down, very gently, in all directions.

James climbed to the top of the little mound, like an upside-down pudding basin that rose in the middle of the grassy space, and looked round again. He saw the green speck of the bus far away, coming along the line of the Huntingdon road, among the other toy cars and tiny lorries.

'I'm fed up with this,' he said to Angey. 'Let's go home.'

'O.K.,' she said.

They collected James's muddy bike, and trotted back.

'You din't oughter be scared of Terry,' she said, as they regained the village street.

'Terrific,' said James. 'Why not?'

'He only likes you if you're not scared of him,' she said.

'Big deal,' said James. 'So what about you?'

'I'm scared of him,' she said. 'That's why I'm not in his gang. He don't like it. He looks after me, so he reckons I got no right. But what he don't see is how I'm scared of everyone, almost. Tisn't just him.'

'Don't tell me,' said James, 'almost everyone, but not me, right?'

'Well, who could be scared of you, bor?' she said. 'Can I come home with you and watch your telly?' When he didn't answer she said, 'Go on, it's nearly time for "Play-school". I like that.'

'What's wrong with watching on your own telly?' he asked, but he guessed what she would say before she said it.

'We haven't got one. That's broken, and that costs too much to mend.'

'Oh, all right,' he said, grudgingly, 'But I'm not watching kids' stuff. You'll have to watch it by yourself.'

James's father came in through the front door just as Angey left, full of buns and rice pudding, and biscuits, which his mother had offered. James had watched with increasing gloom. Feeding Angey was probably like feeding a stray cat he thought – once you started you couldn't stop.

His father had a white paper roll under his arm, and was looking pleased.

'Got something to show you,' he said, and unrolled his paper on the kitchen table, disarraying the set of knives and forks and mats for supper. He had brought a large-scale Ordnance Survey map of the village. It showed The Terrace clearly, and even the outlines of the tiny gardens. Mother pored over it, leaning beside Father. James, who had not joined in Angey's tea, wondered how long supper would be delayed.

Then his father said, 'Look, it shows the Post Office in a different place.'

'When you come to think of it,' said Mother, 'that's where the telephone box is.'

'Is it an old map?' said James, suddenly interested. He wriggled between his parents, to get a look. The Post Office was marked by the bottom of the path, and, he saw at once, the map named the path Mill Drove. He followed it with a finger ... almost at the edge of the sheet – the map got very little in – was an outline of a windmill. It was just where the mound was that James had stood on with Angey. Away from it ran the three tracks, just dotted lines, each called path. But the fourth, the one you would turn right on, was called Samson's Lane. It ran off the edge of the map immediately.

'Where's the next map?' asked James.

'They cost enough,' said his father. 'I only bought the one with us on it. What's for supper?'

While they were eating, the crunch of gravel on the path at the back announced the Home-Help lady, departing. Mother got up from the table, and went to the back door, and called her.

'How is he tonight?' she asked.

'Don't know how he does it,' Mrs Parsons could be heard saying. 'He oughtn't to be here at all by what I'm told . . .'

The kitchen door was closed on James and Father and Mother's voice and Mrs Parsons's murmured on a while behind it.

'Tomorrow,' James thought, 'I really will find it tomorrow.'

The next day Scarf cornered James in the changing rooms after the football game. 'You watch out, bor,' he said. 'Don't go rampaging about on that bike after school today, right?'

'Wrong,' said James. 'If I've got somewhere to go I'm going, and if I've got something to do, I'm doing it.'

'Well, don't say I never telled you,' said Scarf.

But after school James fetched the bike from the shed, and set out. On the mill mound Angey was waiting for him.

'You again,' he said. 'Terrific.'

'You might need some help,' she said, jumping up and coming over to him.

'Can you fight?' said James, bitterly.

They went down the path the map called Samson's Lane, gently descending past orchards. In Yorkshire a slope like this would have been called dead flat, but here it seemed considerable. 'Cambridgeshire Alps, this is,'

James murmured to himself. On one side the orchard screened them, and on the other a thick hedge, noisy with birds. At the foot of the slope, and across the road, lay a dyke full of green water, with a plank bridge laid across it, and beyond that they scrambled up a steep bank. Beyond the bank was the fen. It was a wide, wide flat expanse, divided by a bank running to join the one they were standing on. On one side lay a deeply sunken field, planted with green, growing rows; on the other a field at a higher level, covered deep in rank growth of plants and flowers. Far off, beyond the fen, was a glint of river.

'Well, that's it,' said Angey. 'Now what?'

'Now we're supposed to find a ruined cottage,' said James.

'I never seen one here,' said Angey.

'Mostly fallen down, but just sticking up a bit ...' James quoted the Gaffer.

'Well, if it isn't sticking up very far, it'll be lower than the plants,' said Angey, with her usual grip. They stood and scanned the endless view. So much distance and so much sky made it dazzling, whichever way you looked, as though all directions at once were towards the sun. And James couldn't see anything special. Thick, fleshy plants, not kinds James knew, covered the fen to knee height, or to waist height here and there. The plants cast shadows, and some bore flowers, so that looking for a speck of a different colour was hopeless.

James stared with a sinking heart.

'We could follow the path,' said Angey. 'If the path used to go to the cottage, then if we looked each side of the path we might strike lucky.'

There was a path. It looked no more than a trodden swathe, meandering towards the river. 'Can't see what else we can try,' James agreed.

They waded into the flowery depths. James one side, Angey the other, each a yard or two away from the path, they beat around through the growth. Pale tiny butterflies fluttered up as they thrashed their way along. It was slow going. It was worse than slow, it was hopeless. Miles in every direction stretched the thick plant cover of the luxuriant fen. It would take an army of people working for a week to find something on all that.

Half way to the river James stopped. 'This isn't any good, Angey,' he said, miserably.

'No,' she said.

They turned, as though they had decided to retrace their steps, and saw at once Terry's mob, outlined against the sky, running along the top of the fen bank. Of the tiny, toy-soldier figures, two were already down the bank, and running towards them, far off, along the path. Fright made James move fast. He ran away from the path, tearing his legs through the plants, as though wading. A yard or two, and he knew it was hopeless.

From the bank they could see you wherever you went. They could spot you miles away ... Suddenly the hopelesss difficulty of finding the Gaffer's chimney stump and the hopeless difficulty of going unseen on the fen clicked together in James's brain.

'Lie down, Angey!' he called. 'Just lie down!' and he threw himself full length into the damp embrace of the deep weeds.

In a while he rolled over. He was lying in a shallow,

James-shaped depression in the growing surface of the land. He looked at sky, sky grass-fringed, and with a sound of larks high above. There was a smell of plants. The little pale moths brushed against his face, and the sun seemed suddenly fiercely warm, as he lay out of the wind going over the top of the plants, and keeping them swaying and dipping. The voices of Terry's mob came nearer, then very near, and passing him, and then faint and far away again.

'Angey?' said James. 'You all right?'

There was no answer, and James simply didn't dare sit up and look for her. He lay still, for ages.

Later he woke up very stiff, and sat up before he remembered why he was lying down, or where he was. The world was empty of pursuit; no one in sight except Angey, coming along the path.

'I came back to tell you they've all gone fishing,' she said. 'I told them you'd gone home.'

'Angey, what am I going to do?' he said. 'I'll have to go in and see the Gaffer, and tell him I haven't found it, and he'll be dreadfully upset. And I *can't* tell him I can't find it; I can't bear to!'

'We could keep looking,' she said. 'No. It's no use. We need to know where it was, roughly. Tell you what, my gran might know that. We'll have to ask my gran. Come along then!'

'Now?' asked James.

'Thought you was in a hurry,' said Angey.

'Will she mind?'

'She's a bit strange, my gran. You'll have to take her how you find her, that's all.'

66

They found her trying to change the tubing from one gas bottle to another outside her van, and cursing horribly. James started well, by trying to shift the nut for her, and managing it. Angey's gran climbed into the trailer, talking about making tea.

'Gran, do you remember Samson's place, down on the fen?' said Angey. 'I'll make the tea. This is James.'

'James,' said Angey's gran, sounding, James thought, cross. 'Yes, I remember it. Not senile yet, am I? What about it?'

'Where was it?' asked Angey. 'Is there any milk?'

'Drink it black or go without,' said Gran. 'It was on the rodden, wasn't it? Had to be.'

'What's a rodden?' asked James. Angey's gran looked at him severely. 'You've been helping Angey with her sums,' she said, as though she were accusing him of breaking windows. 'A rodden, thass a ribbon of hard sandy land going across the peat. Just a bit raised up, that is. If you put houses on peat they tip over after a bit, like a van with a wheel broke, so folk put 'em on the rodden where they'll stay standing.'

'We didn't see one of those today,' said James.

'Easy to see in winter, or when they plough,' she said. 'All overgrown come spring, come summer. Along the rodden, somewhere, that's where it was. Wass it to you?'

So James told her. He told her about the Gaffer and his luck, and what the gipsy girl had said about it, years and years ago, and how the Gaffer wanted it back, and how James was supposed to find it . . . he unburdened himself of it all.

67

'You've got a job on there,' said Angey's gran when he had done. 'You could do it in winter.'

'He can't wait that long,' said James sadly. 'He's starting to hurt.'

'Gran, why was Samsons' right down in the fen?' said Angey, pouring dark tea.

'They was fishers and fowlers, Samsons. Had a decoy pond. Lived near the job, that's why. The last great drowned came up and covered everything. Everything flooded. Drove them out. There wasn't much of a living left in ducks by then anyway. They come up into the village, and took that cottage in the malting. That year the water came right down the High Street, but it never came into the maltings front doors. Old Mrs Samson liked to think of that.'

James thought the conversation was going off the point. 'The trouble is,' he said, '*telling* him I can't find it.'

'I'll come with you,' said Angey's gran. 'I'll tell 'im!'

James wasn't at all sure this was a good idea, but he didn't like to say so. So he found himself leading Angey and her gran past his own back door, and into the Gaffer's cottage, hoping his mother wouldn't look out and see them on the way.

'You old fule!' said Angey's gran, the moment she got into the Gaffer's room. 'You die if you want to, bor, ain't nothing stoppin' yer.'

'Oi just wants it back,' said the Gaffer. 'Wass wrong with that? Thass mine, in't it? I can ask furr it if I want to!'

'You can ask for it, but you can't have it, thass all,' she said.

'The boy'll get it for me,' said the Gaffer. 'He said he would. Wass it to you?'

'You just listen to me, you poor criter,' said Angey's gran, sitting down in the chair like one invited, while James and Angey listened horrified in the door. 'You

don't want to believe all that. You don't want to believe all that twattle. Tell you anything, gipsies will. Thieve from your back, and lie to your face, anything for a bit of good. Tell you moonshine for a turnip, us will, never mind for a rabbit. Little ones is *always* hungry, and big ones too. You don't want to mind a words what's said; you been diddled, thass all.'

She stopped. The Gaffer lay looking at the ceiling, and didn't answer her.

'This is Angey's gran, Gaffer,' said James, choking with embarrassment, and feeling responsible.

'I know who she is,' the Gaffer said.

'Well I'm off,' said Angey's gran, getting up as abruptly as she had sat down. 'But anything you're doing, you just git on with it, old man. Don't mind what nobody told you.'

She marched out. Angey followed her, but James stayed. 'Sorry about that,' he said. 'I can't find your cottage, Gaffer. I thought she might help me.'

'Can't find it?' said the Gaffer. 'Used to be able to see the chimney . . . In't it there no more?'

'Can't see it now.'

'It's a year or two since I were down there,' said the Gaffer. 'Keeps on changing. Can't keep track of it. Dear oh dear. Makes you think every minute will be your next. You better quit then, bor. You better go fishing or what.'

James should have been pleased, being let off. But he heard himself saying, 'No. I'll keep trying. Tomorrow's Saturday; I'll have a bit more time.'

'You're a good boy, you are,' said the Gaffer. 'And

your mam's no trimagant, neither. That rice pudding she give me wasn't the best I ever eaten, but it was just like it!'

'I'll tell her,' said James.

But on the next day it rained. Not just ordinary rain, but a determined continuous barrage from dawn to dusk. James did make a half-hearted attempt to go out, but his mother protested vehemently. He lay under his skylight, watching raindrops splatter, fuse and flow, drawing a shifting pattern of distortion across a prospect of blue-black cloud. When watching rain on glass palled, James rolled over and read comics.

He ate too much at lunch, from sheer boredom, and fell asleep feeling sick in the afternoon. Then he was cross and crochety all evening.

'For heaven's sake, let it be dry tomorrow!' his mother said. 'I can't take another day of James indoors.'

But the next day was just the same. And the next. It poured with rain steadily, all week. Mother sent James to the cinema in Cambridge, just to get him out of the house. Of course she paid for Angey to go too. They got wet to the skin just between the cinema and the bus station, coming home, and arrived back cold and shivering, and in need of instant hot baths. Angey didn't seem to fancy a bath, so Mum drove her home while James lay soaking sleepily. The weather forecast said it would rain again tomorrow, and that it was the wettest April on record. Mother went to see the Gaffer every day; James hadn't the heart.

He had the Gaffer on his mind, though. He woke up in the middle of the night, thinking about him. His skylight was silent; no drumming, no pattering, no hissing. Instead, above the dry glass were moistly winking stars. James got out of bed, and looked out of the window. A pale moonsilvery light shone on everything. Drifting white mists floated over the distant levels. The rain had stopped at last. Downstairs his parents would be asleep; but if he called out, they would come. They would wake up, and come stumbling up to see what was wrong. He had only to raise his voice. Their nearness wrapped round his mind like a blanket against the chill and ghostly outside night. But in the Gaffer's house there was nobody except him. Nobody he could call. If he was dying, he would die all alone. The thought clutched at James. He knew at once he would have to go and see how the Gaffer was. He picked up his shoes, and began to tiptoe down the stairs.

He put on the light downstairs to find his anorak by, to slip it over his pyjamas, and at once realized that the Gaffer's cottage would be pitch dark. He wouldn't be able to see if the old man was all right, without waking him up. James looked at the kitchen clock. Two-thirty. No time to go waking neighbours up. James thought for a moment, and then went to the dresser drawer and took a white candle, the sort his mother kept for electricity cuts. He took the box of matches from beside the stove. He unbolted the back door and crept out, candle in one hand, matches in the other. He could not step so softly his footfalls made no sound on the gravel, but he tried. He scrunched the path very softly as he went, creeping along by the wall, with his faint moonshadow creeping just ahead of him. In the Gaffer's little sentry-box porch he struck a match and lit the candle.

Then he felt afraid to go in. What if the Gaffer was dead? What would dead look like? At last he lifted the latch slowly, not to make a click, and slipped past the door-curtain into the Gaffer's room. A dull glow of embers in the fireplace was the only light, but James's candle shone enough for him to see the Gaffer by. The old man was lying on his back, very straight in the bed. His eyes were closed; they were sunk in their sockets and rimmed all round with the jut of bone just beneath the skin. The bones of his cheek and jaw stood out, heavily shadowed in the candlelight.

'What in tarnation dew yew think you'm at, outer bed this time of night?' said the Gaffer suddenly. James jumped so he nearly dropped the candle. He hadn't seen the Gaffer's eyes open.

'I came to see you were all right,' he said.

'I have been better, that I can say,' said the Gaffer. 'But I don't need no candle-traipsing gooing on. You get back to bed, bor.'

'But are you just lying there, wide awake with your eyes shut?' asked James.

'Wass wrong with being awake?' said the Gaffer. 'What about yew, then? Yew fast asleep, are you, wandering about with a candle? I'm thinking, bor. I got a lot to think on.'

'Can I fetch you anything?' asked James. 'Do you want a drink of water?'

'I'nt going to be any shortage of water,' said the

Gaffer, chuckling. 'There'll be short drinking at the Vicky Arms.'

'Whatever are you on about now, Gaffer?' asked James. 'I don't understand the half of what you say.'

'That pub down on the crossroads,' said the Gaffer. 'Us uster sit in there in our Wellington boots, and the water would come up so fast you couldn't finish your pint. You'd be in there with your boots on, and you'd go wading out with your pint half drunk!'

'I still don't know what you're on about!' said James.

'Well, I ain't talking to you, bor. I'm a-talking to myself, see.'

'And why do you keep calling me "bor"?' demanded James, exasperated.

'Thass "bor" like "neighbour", boy, not "bore" like a long sermon. And you oughter be in bed.'

'Yes,' said James. 'I'm going now. Good-night.'

'Good tomorrer morning, more like.'

'And you'll be all right?'

'I ain't gooing to be all right again, bor. I'm whoolly wore out. Me legs hurt, and me chest hurts. But I ain't a-gooing nowhere without you fetch me luck. I'll still be here thinking when I'm a hundred and something and you're grown up, else.'

'But Angey's gran said . . .'

'What does she know about anything?' said the Gaffer. 'She's a gipsy, she is. Tell you anything, they will.'

'But . . .' James began, and then, baffled, he stopped. 'It'll be dry tomorrow. I'll try some more.'

'Dry?' said the Gaffer. 'Five foot deep, more like. Goo off home, bor, and let's get some sleep.'

James stepped outside into the cool, dimly shining night. He blew out the candle, and crept back all the way to bed.

He slept late. A bright fair morning did not wake him at once. When he did get up, realizing with a lift of the heart that the rain really had stopped, it was to a sense of strangeness. The sloping ceiling above his head seemed unusually lit, bright, soft. There was no direct sunshine in the room, just brightness. For a moment, sleepily, James thought of snow, of snowlight all oddness and shadowless glare. But it wasn't snow, of course, in May. Mist, rather. Looking up from his window he saw a bright blue cloudless sky, full of the promise of sunshine; looking down he saw the fields and meadows spreading between home and school gently steaming. Swathes of white mist rolled off them, rose, and drifted. The wet land was drying in the sun, like wet clothes in front of the fire, making a mist-drift far and wide. And something else; there was a brightness somewhere, a snowlight though not of snow, something different, a grounded radiance. The little flake of gold that was the St Ives church weathercock glinted across the veiled meadow, though it wasn't usually struck bright by the morning sun. James shook his head. Probably he had just forgotten what it was like when it wasn't raining.

Half way downstairs he heard his mother's voice, saying, 'That's funny, Peter. I'm sure I locked up last night; did you go out again for something?' He nipped into the bathroom, to allow the conversation to move on before he appeared. By the time he got down his parents were about to go shopping.

'Dad?' said James. 'Can I borrow your binocliars?'

'Binoculars,' said his father. 'Yes. Don't drop them.'

James got them from the coat peg where they hung, and took them up to his bedroom window. He contemplated the weathercock through them. It was glinting; a half-light, moonshine sort of glint, not the full gold of the full sun. And it was facing the wrong way in the wind to be shining at all. Odd. But it was fun looking through the binoculars. James found the school windows with them, and was that someone's football lying in the flowerbed below the window, half hidden? It was miles away! Then he thought of scanning steadily across the flowers of the fen, looking for a chimney-stack ... He ran downstairs.

He wouldn't have stopped for breakfast, but a note from his mother propped against the marmalade jar told him to look in the oven, and he found a plate of bacon and eggs. Then it seemed a pity not to have toast. When he got outside the mist was almost gone, the sun was shining through the thinnest muslin hanging in the air, and it was beginning to be warm. He put the binoculars in the handlebar basket, and rode off on the Gaffer's bike.

And looking down from the mill mound, when he reached it, he saw the source of shining in the morning. The sky lay all below him as well as above. The sky had swung down, and lay outspread, mirrored on the levels beyond the dyke, with the trees growing up through it, their soft green cloud of fresh leaf reflected, repeated below them, and the clouds light-rimmed, gleaming in the heights and in the depths. The fen was under flood-water, for miles and miles. The river was nowhere: the river was everywhere. The air sky and the water sky fused seamlessly on the horizon. And the world shone above, below, and from edge to edge.

Dazzled, James left his bike, took the binoculars, and trotted down the path. He climbed the bank. Strip puddles lay between the cabbage rows on the sunken field; on the other side the water filled the fen bank to the brim. And on the sudden lake were swans resting. A hundred swans, or more maybe. They flocked, floating. They raised their wings to the breathless air. They dipped and curved their slender necks. And their whiteness sang to your eyes across the shining miles.

James shouted out with joy. But it was not for the swans; it was for the island! For there was a dry patch in the flood. A long slender serpentine island had appeared in the fen. For most of its length it was narrow and twisting; the centre stretch was wider. In a moment James had it in the binoculars, picked out. In a moment he had found the broken brick wall, just visible, with the grasses waving round it, higher than the top course, but letting him glimpse. The Gaffer had lived on an island, on the only scrap of land that didn't flood!

The water had no kind of shore. At every edge it was fringed with the common grass and weeds, standing in the water, breaking the surface. James took off his shoes and socks, and waded in a little way. The submerged growth tugged at his ankles. He was in well above his knees in three or four paces. He looked helplessly towards the island. It was many times further off than he had ever swum. Patterns of wind-plucked roughness and of smoothness dappled the surface. Wind, and perhaps the current of the lost and flowing river, taking a course somewhere. It would have to be a boat. James scrambled out again, and put his clinging socks back on his goosey feet.

He met Angey half way back to the mound.

'Where can I borrow a boat?' he asked her.

'There is one kid what has a boat,' she said. 'I don't know nobody else.'

He didn't need to ask who. The pit of his stomach felt heavy. 'There must be somebody else,' he said.

'There's punts for hire at Houghton. And there's day-boats at the trailer park,' she said. 'But they'd never let you have them when the water's up like this. They open all the locks up, and just let the river through, and the boats is all stopped. There isn't going to be a grown-up what will let you have a boat just now.'

They got to his bike, lying in the weeds. James kicked gloomily at the damp grass. 'I can't have a boat till the flood's gone, and I don't need one,' he said.

''Sright,' she said. 'Course, the water goes down quick as it comes up, and you might get to walk there in a week or so.'

'But when we could walk there, we couldn't see where it was,' he said.

'So that's got to be Terry's boat, in't it?' she said, gently.

'He won't lend it to me,' said James. If he was shivering it was only because his feet were damp and frozen numb.

'Can't never tell with Terry,' she said. 'He might. Come on. I'll come with you if you want.'

'Thought you were scared of him,' said James.

'Yes,' she said. 'O.K., I'll wait for you here.'

And James with a sinking heart went off alone.

At the foot of the path, Angey caught up with him. 'Bet you don't even know where Terry lives,' she said.

'No,' said James. 'I don't.'

'Come on,' she said. 'I'll show you.'

It was half way along Mill Lane. An ungated yard opened straight into the street. Two sides of it were enclosed by crazy, leaning creosoted fencing, the other two by the house and its outbuildings. The house, made of common yellow brick with a roof of rusty corrugated iron, looked dilapidated rather than old. Propped in the gateway, a board offered POTATOES BEETS CARROTS SWEATCORN FOR SALE.

'His dad grows all that stuff,' Angey said.

A big dog sprang towards them as they entered the yard, but was pulled up short by a chain. It strained at the chain, barking furiously.

'Shurrup!' came Terry's voice, from the door of an outbuilding. And then, 'What do *you* want?'

'We got something to ask you,' Angey said.

'I'm busy. Come in here.' The shed was full of sacks of various sizes. Terry seated himself at a scrubbed table, on which were a huge pile of carrots, and a weighing machine.

'Give us a carrot!' said Angey.

Terry pushed a carrot across the table. 'Always hungry, you are,' he said. Angey took a huge, muddy

79

bite. 'Give him one, too,' she said, nodding towards James.

'I don't want a carrot,' said James, hastily, 'thank you.'

'You ain't bin offered one,' Terry said. 'What you doing here, anyway? You want to buy something? If you don't, push off!'

'I need to borrow your boat,' said James, 'just for an hour or two.' He felt himself blush hot as he got it out.

Terry stared. 'Oh, you do? Anything else you'd like while you're asking? What do you want it *for*?'

'To get to an island.'

'You're not taking my boat out today. River's not safe in this state. Anyway, why should I lend you my boat? Go and play somewhere else, before I gets narked.'

'I don't want to take it on the river. Only on a bit of flooded fen.'

'Bloody cheek.' Terry filled and weighed three bags of carrots in silence. Then, 'What you waiting for? Nothing doing.'

'Go on, lend him that boat!' said Angey. 'You can't want it today yourself. Your dad'll kill you if you leave off minding the stall.'

'He'll be back soon,' said Terry.

'Well, if we've got the boat off've you before then, I won't be around to tell 'im where you get your money for fags, will I?' said Angey.

Terry scowled, and then, amazingly, he grinned. He took a pretended swipe at Angey. 'Oh, all right,' he said. 'If he really wants it, he can have it for a dare.'

'What's the dare?' said James.

'Ah, ha, ho hum,' said Terry. 'Wouldn't you like to

know? Anything I like. You agree to anything, *anything* I ask you when you bring the boat back. Or else no boat.'

For one short moment James hesitated. Then he re-membered the Gaffer saying, 'I'm starting to hurt ...' 'All right,' he said. 'Done.'

Terry looked pleased, positively gleeful. 'I'll fetch it for you,' he said. 'And I'll lend you the barrer to take it in; it's a bit heavy.' He produced a muddy dark red plastic sack, with a pair of paddles sticking out of the top. 'You can get it inflated at the garage,' he said, 'as long as nobody sees you. The air is round the back.'

'Thank you, Terry,' said James.

'Hum, ha,' said Terry. 'Oh, and another thing. Don't you take Angey out in that boat, or I'll do you over good and proper. She can't swim, can she!'

They played safe, and kept clear of the garage. They borrowed the footpump from the boot of James's mother's car. They trundled the boat in the barrow up the path, down the path, over the dyke, and to the wet rim of the flood. Then they unfolded it, and began to blow air into it. It was positively warm in the sun, and James took off his sweater. Larks trilled and whistled over their heads. The boat looked all right when they got it inflated. It had little rubber rowlocks, and a wooden seat that dropped in amidships. James got in, and Angey pushed him off. It dragged a little at first, weighed down in the clogged and grassy shallows, and then floated free. James dipped the paddles, and set out across the flood.

It was a long way; longer by far than it had looked from the bank. The boat rode lightly and silently, and James soon got the hang of how to paddle it, but the water stretched out behind him, and still stretched far in front. In a while he got among the swans. They seemed large, and dangerous, and one hissed loudly at him. But they swam away from him. When he still rowed on amongst them, the nearest ones took to flight. Their wings beat loudly, like slow sequences of cannonshot, booming over the water. It seemed at first they were too slow and heavy to rise; then the loud wings cleared the water, and the tip of each one just touched at each slow downbeat, leaving behind the mounting outstretched bird a double row of silver ripple-rings, spaced by the rhythm of the wing-strike. The sound of their flight boomed at James's back as he rowed. Behind him, between him and the receding bank, they came to rest again, gliding down on to the flood on a long slide of splashing water, and folding their quiet wings.

Then he was through the swans, and near the island. And then the boat stuck, and grasses tugged and tangled with the paddle blades, and he had run himself aground on the rodden.

He scrambled along to the chimney-stack, what was left of it, crouching in the grasses. There was an angle of fallen wall too, a debris of brick and timber, choked with weed. What had been the floor of the Gaffer's cottage was deep in growth. James looked in bafflement at the grass, at the chimney, three bricks high. Then he tugged hard at the growing weeds. He should have brought a spade; he would have to dig. At the thought of rowing all the way back to land, trekking back home, getting a spade, rowing again, he felt suddenly frantic. 'Does the Gaffer know what he's doing to me, expecting all this?' he thought, desperately. 'I can't. He needs a grown-up . . .'

Suddenly the grass he was tugging at came up in a handful. It came away clean from a surface of reddish tiles. A thick white mat of roots, all woven smooth across the face of the tiles, with the plants growing green up from it, lifted as he pulled and pulled. It was locked down between one tile and the next, wherever it could find a crack to grow down through. But across half the hearth the tiles were solid, and the plant cover came clean away, like a heavy rug lifting, as he tugged and tore it from its entangled edges. And as he cleared the tiles, one came out, tipped and lifted away in a tangle of root. James yelled in triumph, and knelt down to it, and put his hand in the earthy hole it left unlidded. In among the trailing roots, and the sifted earth washed down there, he found a black, soggy rectangle, a greasy rotted package, that fell apart as he got his fingers on it. But with a chink on the tiles, there fell from it the Gaffer's luck – a little black blade of stone, leaf-shaped, and flood-cold, and sharp.

James put it in the money-pocket of his jeans, and zipped it up. Then he went back to the boat.

He saw, as he pushed off, and lurched forward, tumbling himself into the boat, that Angey no longer waited for him alone. All round her were other tiny figures. It would be the whole village gang. Terry and all. James turned his back on them to row towards them. He felt so stone-heavy with dread, he thought he should have sunk, boat and all, down with the drowned flowers, the drowned grass.

Everyone helped deflate and roll up the boat. They took the paddles in two, and packed everything back in bag and barrow, as though they were all friends, and used to helping each other. Then they all looked at Terry, and Terry said, 'I dare you to cross The Rymers.'

'No!' wailed Angey. 'Terry, no!'

'He said he'd take any dare,' said Terry, 'so it's his lookout, in't it? Cross The Rymers.'

'That's a summer dare,' said Scarf, quietly.

'Well, it's May.'

'You know what I mean. The water's up. Wrong time for it, Terry.'

Terry ignored him and looked straight at James. 'You taking this dare, are you?' he said.

'Yes,' said James. 'What's The Rymers?'

'We'll take you there,' said Terry, 'now.'

They trailed in a pack back to the village, and put Terry's boat back in the shed. They picked up James's bike, and Scarf put Angey on the cross-bar of his, and they all went riding out of the village on the other side.

They rode to the upper meadow, as far upstream as the fen was downstream. It lay sodden, the grass and golden dandelions weaving through fragments of water, knitting down broken reflections of the sky. Here and there wide puddles lay, and many of these were across the path. Their bikes ploughed through the pools with arcs of water curving away from the front wheels on either side like wings. They followed the path to the river bank, which stood a few feet higher than the meadow, and was firm and dry. They left their bikes propped along the fence round the lock. The lock gates stood open, and the guillotine top gate was raised and chained. The river broke into a frantic fury and stormed through the open lock, lashing itself white, and roaring as it went.

The gang went on. Along the bank, upstream. You would have said, seeing them, they were a gang of friends, all together, but the togetherness cut out James. They reached a break in the bank they were going along, a small weir, controlled by grey machinery, and with a footbridge across it. Part of the river poured over it into a pool, and ran away to the other side of the meadow, making a backwater. They all crossed the bridge, and went on. The path was thick and deeply grassed now. Willows grew along the river bank, and wild briar tangled along it. Ahead of them, beyond the endless winding trill of the larks, James could hear the deep roar of more water. At last they pushed through a scrubby clump of trees, and came to another weir. This one ran long and straight along the river bank. The glassy surface of the river curved over it smoothly, and ran down unbroken over the concrete slope. At the foot of the slope it broke, curved right back over itself and frothed and fumed a stained and furious white. Across the top of the weir was a row of stout posts, made of angle-iron, standing in the water, and carrying slack lengths of heavy iron chain. Each stretch of chain dipped into the water in the middle of its span, and carried a festoon of taut slimy weed. The wide pool into which the weir fell was choppy and angry for yards and yards below the water-slide. This pool too discharged into a backwater, and made its own way across the meadow, diverging from the parent stream.

'This is The Rymers,' said Terry.

'And that's The Sleeping Waters,' said Ted, indicating the pool, 'only something's woke it up!'

'This is it,' said Terry, looking at James.

'Yes, but look at it, Terry,' said Scarf. 'You can't dare it now. Take it back.'

'Oh, don't be so feeble, Scarf,' said Terry. 'He in't going to *do* it, is he? He's going to funk it.'

James stood on the brink, with everyone watching him.

'You swine, Terry, you sodding swine!' said Angey, and James shook his head, to shake her voice out of his ears, to think clearly.

He was going to funk it. They would trail back along

the bank, in a group that would leave him out. He would always be left out now. They knew he couldn't do that; and yet he would always have funked it. For as long as he lived, he would never be village, never have any friend but Angey here. He *couldn't* funk it. And yet, when he looked at the weir he was terrified. He pushed his mind to think about it; you would lower yourself in over the concrete bulkhead, and hold on by the loosely swinging chain ... his mind bucked away and refused to think about it.

So he did the only thing he knew. He turned round and looked Terry full in the face and said, 'I'll do that when you've done it.'

He didn't know, as he said it, if it would work. But in Yorkshire there had been rules to dares. If you dared someone to do something, you were supposed to be willing to do it yourself. You could have it turned back on you, and then you had to do it first, otherwise the disgrace fell on you.

And it seemed he was right; it seemed that was the rule here too. Someone laughed. 'Not thick, is he?' said Tracy.

'O.K., Terry, let's see yer, then!' said Ted.

'Come on then, old mate, let him off, and let's all get back,' said Scarf. 'I've got some money for chips when the van comes.'

James just had time to wonder what life would be like if you had made a fool of Terry. Would someone else be top? Then he saw Terry wasn't backing down. Terry was taking off his jacket, and giving it to Scarf to hold. Terry was sitting on the edge, and easing himself forward into the water, with one hand on the first length of chain.

'Terry, don't,' said Scarf, softly and urgently, 'it isn't worth it . . .'

Angey let out an ear-shattering wail, wordless and terrified. The others stood around and watched. Terry slid his weight off the wall and stood knee-deep in the surging water, bent over the chain and hanging on hard. He began to ease sideways, sliding first one foot and then the other. But the farther he moved out from the bank, the lower the chain hung and the less support he got from it.

'He's the wrong side of the chain,' James thought, seeing Terry struggle and sway; 'he ought to have it between him and the drop . . .'

It was amazing how far Terry got: somehow to the second post, and half way along the second stretch of chain. Then he lost his footing. He slipped, and hung full length from the chain, in the water to his shoulders, bouncing in the ferocious glide of the water down the slope. For a long minute he hung on to the chain, scrabbling for a foothold, then the water plucked him off and hurled him viciously into the seething pool. They all heard his head crack hard and loud on something. The water rolled him over, sucked him under, and threw him up to the surface again.

Scarf began to run. They all ran. Round the rim of the pool, which took them far from Terry. In a few paces Scarf stopped, hesitated, turned, and plunged in. He swam out into the boiling pool. Shocked and motionless, James watched. Terry was floating, far out, face down. Scarf reached him and rolled him over. The two of them were flung around, thrust across the surface of the pool by the driving water, and dragged towards the stream that flowed away across the meadow. But the rest of the gang were in the water too, now. They had climbed in and were standing, making a human chain across the narrow throat of the outfall. And slowly now, but inevitably, Scarf and Terry were floating towards them. And here came Angey – could she have run all the way to the lock and back again? – with a life-ring on a rope, and running along the bank to meet her, James grabbed it and threw it as hard and as far as he could into the water just beyond Scarf. Scarf bumped into it, and clutched it, and then there were cries, and voices raised, and Terry was dragged out, and up the bank, and laid on the grass.

'We ought to hold him upside down,' said James, remembering lifesaving lessons. Two of the biggest boys picked up Terry by the ankles, and held him just above the ground. James reached out, grasped a handful of Terry's hair, and lifted his head by it. Water ran out of his mouth and nose. Then he drew a great shuddering breath. They put him down again, quickly, and he rolled over a little and was sick on the grass. But James was looking, horrified, at his own right hand. It felt sticky – it was covered in blood. Blood from Terry's hair. 'Look!' he wailed, holding his hand out to Scarf.

'Get someone, quick,' said Scarf, in a funny choked and rattling voice. Angey took off her battered cardigan, and put it round Scarf. 'I've broken my arm,' said Scarf. 'I think I have, because the bone's all sticking through. Don't look.' He was shivering. James didn't want to see Scarf's bone sticking out. He looked at Terry instead. Terry was a funny colour. Every one of his freckles stood

out clearly. His skin was bluish. The side of his head was bleeding slowly, clotting in his hair. He was only a little boy, that was the oddest thing. Lying there bleeding he didn't look dangerous at all, he wasn't much taller than James, and not much older either. He was just a boy, and hurt.

Then, thank heaven!, some grown-ups came. Two fishermen fetched from the river bank. One of them

went off running for the house by the Black Bridge. The children sat shivering in the wet grass. They were all soaked to the skin except James and Angey. It was ages. Ages, and then the ambulance siren sounded, faintly from the direction of the road, and then louder, and very loud. The ambulance men came running across the meadow. They carried Terry away; they would have left Scarf if James hadn't told them about his arm. A worried-looking man had appeared on the scene, who was trying to take them all to his house by the bridge, to get warm. They followed him, silent, avoiding each other's eyes.

'It wasn't James's fault,' piped up Angey, suddenly, ahead of him. 'Terry didn't have to because of James . . .' No one agreed with her. Ahead of them they could see the ambulance men who were now carrying Scarf. The ambulance drove away down the lane from the bridge, its siren wailing. The lane was full of cars; news had travelled, people's parents were coming. In the confusion James walked away, and then found Angey with him. She put a thin arm round him as they walked, and James was glad.

'It wasn't your fault,' she offered again, half way home.

'I think I would die for Scarf, if he wanted me to,' said James, when they reached the gates of the trailer park, and he left Angey.

'He's very brave,' she said. 'Me gran says it's because he's stupid!'

'If it wasn't for him I'd be a murderer,' said James, choking.

A car stopped suddenly with a squeal of brakes, the other side of the road. Father had come to look for James and take him home.

'That was Terry's own fault, that was, *thick-top*!' Angey hissed at James. But James knew she was wrong.

James's parents fussed. His father made him take a sip of brandy, which burned and glowed inside him all the way down. His mother made him strip and get into a hot bath. It was true he was cold, to the bone. Part of him warmed up and glowed pink and rosy in the foamy water, but the thinking part of him was still frozen to death.

'A terrible thing to happen,' his mother said, at the foot of the stairs. 'And the boy is worried, Peter, I can tell. See what you can find out.' Then his father's voice, on the phone, muffled.

'Not good, I'm afraid,' his father was telling his mother, as James in dressing-gown came slowly down the stairs. 'The boy has a fractured skull, and is concussed, and unconscious. They can't tell how bad; apparently he has a haemorrhage that would have been worse if he hadn't been so cold; he'll need an operation to remove the blood-clot, and it's touch and go . . .'

'It's not someone James has mentioned,' his mother said. 'Not a friend, I think. But he's terribly upset . . .'

'Natural, if he saw it happen,' said his father. 'Oh, there you are, James. Feel like some supper?'

'Can I have baked beans?' asked James.

'There's a James Bond on the telly tonight,' his mother said. 'Would you like to stay up and watch it?'

James did like. He fell asleep, leaning against his mother's comfortable bulk on the settee, while the great hero was temporarily boring, talking to a blonde.

So he went to bed late, and sleepy.

He woke in the moonlight, suddenly knowing what to do. 'I'll do that when you've done it,' he had said to Terry. And Terry had done it; the rules didn't say you had to succeed, only that you mustn't funk it. So now it was up to James. Earlier in the day he had been terrified of the weir; now he knew there were worse things, and he had a choice. His father often said, talking about climbing and fell-walking, that people got into trouble because they rushed at things, and didn't take time to think. So James took time to think. He sat in the pool of moonlight on the attic floor, and thought about the weir. He thought of the rush of water, knee-deep, or deeper, the slack chain, the slimy sill beneath. Then he got his climbing boots out of the cupboard. The row of heavy studs on the soles glinted in the cold silver light.

Now. It would have to be now. Tomorrow the flood might have gone down a bit, the fierceness of the weir abated. But if he did it the same day, the same night, there could be no arguing about it. James looked out of the window. The world was dim, but clear. Shadow spires stood into a faint sky. A bright full moon was shining in a cloudless night, littered with brilliant stars. Just the same, he would need a torch. He crept about barefoot, finding his clothes. He had to retrieve his jeans from the airing cupboard, where his mother had put them to dry. He took a boot in each hand, and crept down the stairs.

His bike was still propped on the fence beside the lock; he would have to walk. He tiptoed across the gravel, for fear the crunch would wake someone. In the street he sat on the kerb beneath a lamp-post, and put on his boots, and laced them up. Then he set off for the trailer park.

Angey woke easily; one or two taps on the pane, and there she was, yawning, and dressed. Now he came to think of it, she looked as if she slept in her clothes.

'You don't have to,' she said, at once.

'Yes, I do,' he said. 'But I need someone to see me, or they'll never believe us. Can you get someone?'

She nodded. 'I'll get my trainers, and I'll be right with you,' she said.

They went to Tracy's house first. Angey thought Tracy slept downstairs, but they woke an angry dog before they woke her. Next they tried Ted. James thought wistfully of Scarf, but Scarf was kept in hospital, Angey said. She threw a light handful of grit at Ted's window, and in a while he put his head out. 'Coming,' he said when he saw them, but he seemed to take hours. James got desperate, waiting for him.

'I can't wait, Angey,' he said. 'I've just got to go and do it. Bring anyone you can, O.K.?'

The road through the village, under the tall trees was dark. The lamp-posts were still on, but the limited dim pools of light they made failed to meet each other. James had no idea what time it was, he hadn't brought his watch. No point in wrecking a good watch. He picked his way by torchlight between the pools of lamplight. His boots rang and clattered on the road. And he felt like a thief going by; anyone who saw him would stop him. At last he crossed the bridge, thudding over the planks, and came into the open, gleaming meadow. Threads of silver, broken shards of moon lay in the ghostly grass. He marched on regardless through the pools on the path, to the bank. He did not look at the lock, he couldn't afford to. Hearing the solid roar of the river through it was bad enough. As he crossed the first weir he couldn't help looking where the water ran as hard as ever, leaping and shouting to the distant and disinterested stars.

And then he trudged through the bushes, and was there.

The river gave off a steely glint as it curved over the slope. Were the chains hanging just above the water instead of just into it? James dared not consider now, or stop to think. Instead he turned his back on the river, and lowered himself into the water, going in very deliberately on the riverward side of the chain.

He had expected more depth; it came up to his knees, no more. He had not expected the weight and force of its thrust. It was so cold his skin burned intensely, he felt the violent flushing of his body all over, but he was hanging on to the first post. He felt for the sill, the concrete edge below the water, and carefully hooked the first row of studs on his boots over the lip. He picked up the chain, lifted it over his shoulders, and leaned back into it, pushing against the thrust of the water. Then he began very slowly, holding himself rigid and leaning backwards with all his might, to slide sideways.

As long as he kept leaning against the weight of the water, as long as he didn't let it push him forward, and topple him over the chain, he would be all right. The warm flush of his skin ebbed away leaving him trembling and gasping from cold. Somehow he had eased himself along the first length of chain. As he moved towards the middle it got harder, and he leaned back so far he was looking straight up at the icy stars. He got to the second post. Then he found he couldn't move; he was clinging on to it frantically, terrified of going on, and terrified of going back while his mind replayed to him the sight of Terry being plucked off the chain and flung away. 'But you can't stay,' he told himself. 'You'll get tired, and get washed off, so *move*!' Slowly he unclenched the grip of his right hand, and transferred it to the next length of chain.

He was right in the middle of the weir now, hanging on to the central chain, and fighting for his balance. The water was immense, ruthless. It pushed him forward, and he fought with all the thrust in his frozen limbs to keep himself leaning away from the water-slide, to keep his boots locked over the sill, while the water roared around his knees, and tried to tear his feet from under him. He slid his boots along the sill; he reached the next post. Above the sound of the water, faintly, something reached him; birdlike sounds, voices, calling. He had no mind to spare for that. Somewhere between the third and fourth posts he lost his footing; the sill was crumbling and rough, and he couldn't slide his boots along it. For a moment he teetered, closed his eyes, and gave up. His body flinched all over at the thought of the drubbing and knocking it would take, being dashed down into the pool; and then somehow he had recovered his posture, and was leaning outwards in the loop of chain again. And the force of the water was lessening now with every step he took. He was reaching the lee of the other shore.

The water sped past this length, and turned sideways moments later as though it did not know at first that it was free to go over. Even so, James, suddenly aching and mortally tired, hardly managed the last few steps to the bank. And there he hung on, leaning on the last post, and barely able to drag his soaking body out of the water, and roll himself on to the bank.

Dimly he heard shouting. His name, being called. He

looked back across the shining terrifying moonsilvered stretch of water. Like a solitary glow-worm the torch was dancing. Someone had found it lying on the bank, and was waving it. The shadows in the willows on the other side, moved, and called his name. Lots of shadows. Angey had brought the whole village mob out to watch him.

'James!' they were calling, 'are you all right?'

He lurched to his feet. 'How do I get back?' he called.

'Follow your bank round to the bridge,' yelled Ted.

They walked with him. The torch danced and circled and lit flickering fires in the river between as their shadows marched along the other bank. Stumbling and slow, James walked all alone on his side, and the river puckered, and glittered, and eddied, and harassed the reflected moonlight all the way.

They had picked up their bikes, and someone had brought James his. When they met at the bridge it was engulfed in a rising cold mist, which swirled around them as they slapped James on the back.

'We didn't think you'd make that,' said Tracy.

'Neither did I,' said James through chattering teeth.

As they reached the village street the street lights suddenly went out. The moon sailed behind a bank of cloud. The mist seemed to take courage at once, and thicken, and they couldn't see each other's faces. Laughing a little as they stumbled along in the dark, they passed one door after another, parting whispering from one of the party after another, till James went on alone.

He dragged his sodden boots off, and left them in the porch. The dully glowing embers of a fire were still alive in the grate of the living-room fire. James held out his hands to the warmth, and then stretched out thankfully on the hearthrug, and went at once to sleep.

He woke at first light, cold, and aching, and happy. His clothes had dried on his body, and felt as stiff as boards. He ached in every muscle with each move he made. And he felt as light as air. The sun shone through the thin curtains. Cautiously he stood up, feeling as he did so a hurt keener than the others on his thigh – something pressing there hard enough to be sore. He prodded with his fingers, and found the Gaffer's luck, still zipped into his jeans' pocket. He had been lying on it, and it had pressed hard into his flesh. 'After all that,' thought James, 'I forgot to take it to him.' So he went.

Out along the gardens, in a thick deep morning dew. Birds singing, and a lemon-curd-coloured early sky. The rose bushes in the Gaffer's weed-engulfed garden had unfurled plum-red leaves. James lifted the latch of the always-unlocked door, and went in.

'Good morning, bor,' said the Gaffer, at once, from the bed. He was lying, as always, on his back, propped up on a stack of pillows.

'I brought it,' said James, simply, holding out the little blade of stone. 'This is it, isn't it?'

The Gaffer took it, turned it slowly in his palm, and sighed. 'Hin't changed as much as I have,' he said. 'Hin't changed at all. Thass it, all right, bor. Thass it. You'm a good boy, best neighbour a man could have. Right. So now I got that again, I'm a-giving that to you. Thass your'n now. But you mind, you take notice, mind. Lose that and die quick. Keep that and come to no harm. Give that away, and you get your chances like anyone else. You got that, bor?'

'I've got it,' said James. 'But ...'

'But me no buts,' said the Gaffer. 'Give me your hand here, and have it for yours. And see here, young James. Don't keep that as long as I done. 'Tain't wise.'

'No,' said James. 'I mean, yes. Thank you.'

'Thass my place to thank you,' the Gaffer said. 'I got my chances back. That hasn't been good, a-lying here, and thinking every minute will be my next!'

'You've got that wrong, Gaffer,' said James. 'You

mean thinking every minute will be your *last*, I think. That's what people say.'

'Ah,' said the Gaffer. 'Is that it? Off you goo, bor, I can't talk no more now. Sound like an old fen nightingale already.'

'What's a fen nightingale?' said James. 'I'm going.'

'Frog, you higorant boy,' said the Gaffer, hoarsely. 'Frog.'

It looked ordinary enough, lying on James's bedside table. An ancient thing, a likeable thing, that tempted you to pick it up and stroke its dark rippled shape. You could nearly see into it, but not quite. A flood-water sort of colour. But it didn't look magic. It didn't look as if it could stand between you and your chances. On the other hand, James thought, what had his chances been of getting across The Rymers? And the luck had been in his pocket all the time while he did it, though he had forgotten it was there.

He felt comfortable and safe with the luck beside him. He lay resting on his bed, full of breakfast, looking at it. He wanted to keep it. It asked to be kept. But he knew already that he was going to give it away.

He thought he would go and tell the Gaffer that; the Gaffer should know. But he was very tired. He rested and dozed for a couple of hours before he could bring himself to move. It was nearly noon when he came down again. His mother had gone out, and a stack of sandwiches waited for him on the table. He put them in a paper bag, and put the bag in the handlebar basket of the bike. Then he went in to see the Gaffer.

The Gaffer was lying on his side, curled up tightly, his knees almost to his chin. The fire burned brightly; the home help had been in that morning and left everything neat. There was an immense silence and stillness in the room. James didn't think he would disturb the Gaffer; he didn't think he could. The time for telling him things had gone.

'Goodbye, bor,' said James, in so quiet a whisper, he didn't hear it himself.

He went to find Angey. He thought Angey might come with him. She was hanging about outside the shop.

'You don't need me,' she said. She was looking at the ground instead of at him. 'You'll manage that. Easy.'

'But I'd like you to come.'

'No, you wouldn't,' she said.

'What's up, Angey?' he demanded, crossly.

'I told you I was scared of people,' she said. 'Everyone, almost.'

'Except me, remember?'

'Well, I'm scared of you too, now,' she said, sadly. 'I won't be hanging about you no more.'

'But that's *rubbish*!' he said. 'You can't mean it. I haven't changed!'

'Seen from where I am you have,' she said. 'Before you go, bor, buy us a Mars bar!'

'I'll buy you one with my own money if you'll stop this and come with me,' said James.

' 'Sall right. I got the money,' she said. 'Don't worry about me, James. Why should you? Nobody else does, and I bin all right so far.'

'See you then,' said James, emerging from the shop, and giving her the Mars bar.

'If I don't see you first!' she said, grinning, and skipping away.

It took James ages to ride to the hospital. He was stiff and aching and slow, and he stopped to eat his sandwiches under a tree on the way.

He asked the lady behind glass just inside the main door which ward Terry was in.

'No visitors, he's far too poorly,' she said. 'He's going to need a very dangerous operation.'

'I want to know to send him a card,' said James. 'A get-well card.'

'How nice,' she said. 'Address it to D3.'

'Thank you,' said James. He marched out again through the swing-doors, and went round to a side door leading in from the car park. He picked up a large vase of flowers from the table just inside the door, and marched along the corridor with it and into a lift. The lift buttons gave ward letters and numbers for each floor. James found his way.

D3 was a little room. It had a lot of machines and tubes in it, and two beds. Scarf was in one, Terry was in the other.

'Cripes, don't let anyone see you!' said Scarf, when James walked in and put the flowers down on a locker.

'How is he?' said James.

'Here and there. I mean, he comes and goes. Sometimes he's out cold, and sometimes he talks rubbish, and sometimes he makes sense. I'm supposed to try to talk to him when he makes sense, and ring the bell for the nurses if he seems in pain, or tosses about or anything.'

'How's your arm?' asked James. Scarf waved a white lumpen plaster limb at him. 'Doesn't hurt now. This is *boring*. I'm glad you came.'

'I brought something for Terry,' said James. 'Can I talk to him?'

'Try it,' said Scarf.

A tube went into Terry's nose. His head was bandaged. His eyes were shut.

'Terry,' said James. 'Terry, it's me, James. Terry? Terry, I went back to The Rymers, and I got across.'

'You *what*?' said Scarf.

'I crossed The Rymers,' said James. 'Your gang saw me do it.'

James thought Terry hadn't heard him. Terry's eyes stayed shut, but he suddenly grinned.

'Effing lunatic!' he said. 'You're raving bonkers, you are! Scarf? Did you hear that? That's daft enough to be village, in't it?'

'Easy,' said Scarf.

'Terry,' said James, speaking softly because Terry looked so awful, though he felt like shouting and jumping around, 'I got something for you.' He put the Gaffer's luck into Terry's limp hand. 'It's good luck,' he said. 'Only for heaven's sake don't lose it. Losing it turns the luck bad.'

Terry slowly lifted his hand so that he could look at the luck without moving his head and slowly opened his eyes. 'I like that,' he said. 'That's good, that is. Course I won't lose it. Put it in me sponge bag for now, will you?'

'You can keep it too long, I think,' said James. 'But keep it for now, O.K.?'

'You bet . . .' said Terry. His voice went soft and loud like a radio drifting in and out of tune.

'I don't like to be a wet blanket,' said Scarf, 'but you'd better hop it, James. There'll be hell to pay if they find you here, and they keep coming in and out.'

'James?' said Terry, as he reached the door. James stopped. 'Do something for me, will you, bor?'

'I will if I can,' said James.

'I'll be off school for ages,' said Terry. 'If anyone picks on Angey, fix them for me, will you?'

'If anyone picks on Angey,' said James, 'I'll crunch them up!'

Terry seemed to be smiling faintly, but he didn't answer.

'You make me nervous, hanging about,' said Scarf. 'Terry won't be back for hours now, shouldn't think. Hop it!'

'O.K.,' said James. 'I'll bring you some comics when they let people come.'

'Great,' said Scarf.

James got out into the corridor again. At the top of the stairs was a reception area, with some chairs and a sofa, and more flowers. James sat down, without deciding to.

Then he lay down. He had, for the moment, done everything he could.

Later he was leaning against his mother in the back seat
of the car, being driven home by his father.

'Mr Samson died today, James,' his mother said, seeing
he had woken up. 'Just quietly, in his morning nap.'

'He'll be pleased,' said James, sleepily. 'He wanted that.'
Just the same, he seemed to be crying. His cheeks were
all wet, and the pattern on his mother's shirt was blurry.

'It's been a hard time for you, son, hasn't it? All a bit
too much,' she said, tenderly, holding him close.

And as though he were calling to her across a great distance, James answered, adrift between sleeping and waking, adrift between dreaming and thinking, adrift on the shining floods of chance and time:

'It makes me think every minute will be my next!' he said.

Some other Puffins

TOM TIDDLER'S GROUND
John Rowe Townsend

Vic and Brian are given an old rowing-boat which leads to the unravelling of a mystery and a happy reunion.

A TASTE OF BLACKBERRIES
Doris Buchanan Smith

A moving account of how a young boy copes with the tragic death of a close friend.

COME SING, JIMMY JO
Katherine Paterson

The absorbing story of 11-year-old James's rise to stardom, and the problems of coping with the fans.

BACK HOME
Michelle Magorian

12-year-old Rusty, who had been evacuated to the United States when she was seven, returns to the grey austerity of post-war Britain.

SADDLEBOTTOM
Dick King-Smith

The hilarious adventures of a Wessex Saddleback pig whose white saddle is in the wrong place, to the chagrin of his mother.

THE WHISPERING KNIGHTS
Penelope Lively

Susie, Matthew and William concoct a witch's brew over a fire in an old barn with no real expectation that anything will happen.

FROGGETT'S REVENGE
K. M. Peyton

Danny Froggett is persecuted for being small – until help arrives in the form of Froggett's Revenge, a huge hilarious dog.